CONTENTS

INTRODUCTION 7
THE FERRIS WHEEL   LEO SIMPSON 9
BROTHER AND SISTER   JANE RULE 30
THE STORY OF A CAT   JOHN NEWLOVE 38
A BAUBLE FOR BERNICE   DON BAILEY 45
THE HARBINGER   GEORGE MCWHIRTER 57
MAGICIANS   BETH HARVOR 64
ONE FOR THE ROAD   JOHN SANDMAN 75
THE YEAR   NORA KEELING 92
THE MILL   ANDREAS SCHROEDER 96
THE MAN WHO KILLED HEMINGWAY   GAIL FOX 102
WHO CAN AVOID A PLACE?   DAVID MCFADDEN 112
THE GRAVE OF THE FAMOUS POET
    MARGARET ATWOOD 122
CONTRIBUTORS 134

PR
9196
.S5
H4

Edited by David Helwig & Joan Harcourt
for Oberon Press

72727272
27272727
72727272
27272727
72727272
27272727
72727272

NEW CANADIAN STORIES

KALAMAZOO VALLEY
COMMUNITY COLLEGE
LIBRARY

Copyright © 1972 by Oberon Press
Reprinted 1972
All rights reserved: no part of this book may be
reproduced in any form or by any means, electronic or
mechanical, except by a reviewer, who may quote
brief passages in a review to be printed in a newspaper
or magazine or broadcast on radio or television
Library of Congress Catalogue Card No. 72-77030
ISBN 0 88750 066 8 (hardcover)
ISBN 0 88750 067 6 (softcover)
Book design by Michael Macklem
Printed in Canada by The Hunter Rose Company
PUBLISHED IN CANADA BY OBERON PRESS

INTRODUCTION

Fourteen Stories High, the first of what has become an annual collection of new Canadian stories, was undertaken in the belief that many good stories were being produced in this country, and in the knowledge that it was difficult to place them. The success of the first collection has proved that there is also an interested audience, and uncovered, as well, a great many people writing in this form. The submissions received by the editors for the second anthology numbered close to a hundred, and came from writers from Newfoundland to British Columbia. Nor was the final selection of stories to be included in this volume an easy matter. The general quality of writing was high, and several good stories had to be left out for lack of space.

It is worth noting that, after two years and the publication of 23 writers, it is still possible to list Canadian story writers who, for one reason or another, haven't yet appeared in one of the books: Alice Munro, Dave Godfrey, Austin Clarke, Audrey Thomas, John Metcalf, Clark Blaise, Hugh Hood and David Lewis Stein come easily to mind. Eventually, we hope, our net will catch them all—and others, as yet unknown to the public.

Only three of last year's contributors have been chosen again this year, and these three, Don Bailey, Nora Keeling and Andreas Schroeder are all writers who weren't widely known for their fiction before the publication of *Fourteen Stories High*, though Schroeder was known as a poet, especially on the West Coast, and Don Bailey's journalism and poetry has had some currency in eastern Canada.

One of the remarkable features of this year's collection is the number of poets among the contributors: Margaret Atwood, Gail Fox, David McFadden, George McWhirter, John Newlove and Andreas Schroeder all have established reputations as poets. This is, perhaps, a reflection of a tendency among Canadian publishers over the past few years to be more open to new poetry than to new fiction. Yet, whatever the pressures of publishing, it is clear that many young writers, and those who are just now entering the period of their literary maturity, are not content to be anything less than wholly "writers," men and women who will use their imagination and verbal skill in any form they choose.

DAVID HELWIG/JOAN HARCOURT

THE FERRIS WHEEL

Leo Simpson

"I am, after all, seeking only to establish the correct business relationship," said Harry Merryweather, the plaintiff.

"This seems a simple enough problem," said Edward Seager, the personnel director, the judge. "You, Mr. Merryweather, would like Mr. Grayson to stop calling you Harry, and to address you either as 'Mr. Merryweather' or 'sir.' But you wish to continue to address Mr. Grayson here as George. Is that it? Have I got it right?"

"He's been calling me George for months," George Grayson said, the defendant. "Ever since I joined the company."

"And that's why you feel he should be Harry to you, is it?"

"Sure. What else?"

"I have fifteen years seniority and I'm four scales higher in grade," Merryweather said. "I'm *management*. If you wish, I can cite examples of personnel in my own department who have less seniority, less *grade* seniority, who are addressed with the prefix. And they normally use the given-name address form in their dealings with personnel of George's grade, for instance—"

"That won't be necessary," Seager said. "Let's deal with this case on its merits. Such as they are."

Grayson said: "If he feels friendly enough to call me George, why should he object if I call him Harry? I don't get it."

"Mr. Merryweather?"

"A very important point," said Merryweather. "There's no *friendship*, in fact, in my use of George."

"I don't get it."

"Doesn't Rookes call you George?" Merryweather said. "Sebastian calls you George and Henry Faircliff calls you George. Every one of them gets a prefix from you. It's *Mr.* Rookes, *Mr.* Bolitho, *Mr.* Faircliff."

"Hey, you said Sebastian," Grayson said. "Do you call Mr. Bolitho Sebastian? I'd be interested in an answer to that."

"No, but I should."

"Why is that, Mr. Merryweather?" said Seager.

"Well, on the face of it he's head of his department, I don't deny, and I'm second assistant head of mine. But compare *sizes*. Mine's three times the size, we have three times the work, three times the problems—three times the administrative responsibilities."

"How would it be if I addressed you as Mr. Merryweather and you addressed me as Mr. Grayson?"

"No."

"Couldn't we just avoid the issue altogether? I mean, we don't work that closely together. We could just avoid the issue, Harry."

"Not satisfactory."

"Mr. Grayson," Seager said. "Mr. Grayson, do you feel seriously about this dispute?"

"I don't, indeed. A damn storm in a teacup. I'm doing Harry here a favour by talking about it."

"Then why not let him have his way?"

"Are you serious? You don't know him. He'd make special trips to my office to call me George. I'd see him ten times a day. He'd George me to death in a week. You don't know this one."

"Well, would you gentlemen accept a compromise? How about initials, say? How about addressing each other as, oh, whatever you use, H.M. for you Mr. Merryweather, and G.G. for you Mr. Grayson?"

"No," said Merryweather. "That brings us to the same level again. I want justice."

"Mr. Grayson, what do you say to a small concession? If Mr. Merryweather called you G.G. and you called him Mr. Merryweather?"

"Let me think. I'm wondering if it's just the smirky way he pronounces Jaw-ergh that gets to me. But G.G. is worse, if anything. G.G. sounds horsy."

"Have you a middle name?"

"Yes. Oliver. You get Gog. No."

"It wouldn't do, anyway," Merryweather said. "I'm *entitled* to use George, like the others. And he's got to use Mr. Merryweather, for the sake of the respect."

Grayson said: "Listen, Harry, I don't respect you, even if they make me call you Your Excellency."

"Your feelings aren't important to me, George," Merryweather said. "I don't care what you *feel*."

"Gentlemen, please," said Seager.

"He watches every rotten television show they put on," Grayson said. "He sees every damn episode of *Fugitive Bride* and talks about it the next day. He knows all the commercials, he sings them while he's washing his hands. He never goes to a play, and the only book he's ever read so far as I can tell is *Naked in Newtown*. Respect, for God's sake."

"Mr. Merryweather's personal tastes aren't relevant here," Seager said. "Not a relevant business factor, I believe, at the moment, at least not relevant to this particular argument."

"I don't come back from those outside lunches smelling of vodka," Merryweather said. "Vodka *does* smell, George, for your information. Everybody notices, everybody knows. He hangs around the steno pool, a married man. He's taken that girl with pigtails, Gracie, to lunch twice this week already. How old is she?"

"It's jealousy," Grayson said. "Plain, old-fashioned—"

"Rubbish," said Merryweather. "*You're* jealous. You envy me my position in the company."

"Gentlemen, please."

"How do you figure I envy you, Harry, for God's sake? If I did, wouldn't I envy Mr. Faircliff and Mr. Watson too? But they call me George, and I don't mind. You're the only one who sticks in my craw, Harry."

"You see? He admits it. So where are your staff orders now, Mr. Seager?"

"There are no rules governing this matter in staff orders. We don't go down this far."

"Exactly my point," said Merryweather. "There *should* be. There should be precise rules in staff orders. What have we now? We have people on low grades getting too much respect. Others of definite seniority not getting enough. A mish-mash, instead of a proper chain of command as laid out in the company tree. We need *rules* in the staff order blue-book, clear rules of behaviour governing relations between grades. If you want my opinion, most of the personnel problems we have are caused by this. . .this *confusion*, by this lack of respect, which weakens the chain of command."

Seager said: "Most of the personnel problems we have are caused by people asking for more money, Mr. Merryweather."

"You know best, of course. But my point is that proper rules on such things as surnames and prefixes, and even *attitude*, would bring more efficiency. We need discipline. Every organization needs discipline to function, that's obvious enough surely."

"Mr. Merryweather," Seager said. ". . .Mr. Merryweather, you're wandering a little into my own area of experience there, you're touching on ideas that come inside my scope of knowledge. The trouble with obvious remedies, usually, is that they also have obvious disadvantages. We could very simply set up a flogging-post in general clerical too, for example, but—"

"It just seems to me *surprising* that there are no rules—"

"We're always prepared to listen to fresh viewpoints about efficiency," Seager said. "However, I feel maybe it would be helpful, Mr. Merryweather, if you looked on the dispute with Mr. Grayson as your own problem—I mean, as your personal problem, and not as a flaw in the organization of the company. I'd like to try to settle it on that basis."

"Smarten up, Harry," said Grayson.

"Though my instincts at the moment are in your favour, Mr. Merryweather," Seager said. "When the company promotes a man, it's an expression of respect for his ability. We do expect all staff to agree with our decisions. The implications favour you."

"Then why—"

"What about Rusty?" Grayson said.

"Rusty Bracken. I see," said Seager. "Yes, I do indeed see what you mean, Mr. Grayson."

"Vice-President in charge of Sales Division, four departments," said Grayson. "Nobody calls him Mr. Bracken. He'd be insulted. The mail-boys call him Rusty."

"Well, but he's a special case," Merryweather said. "He came up as a salesman. The very best, of course, but he isn't what you'd call the executive *type*, is he? Rusty's still basically a salesman and he just enjoys selling, he'll never be anything else. A big red-haired salesman, that's Rusty Bracken, an *informal* man, I don't suppose he's even had the formal ed—yes, and not too interested in anything outside his own division. He'd be the first to admit, if you want my—"

Grayson said: "He's on the Board."

"Oh certainly he's on the *Board*, but use your head. *Rusty Bracken*. For crying out loud. May I know what the notebook's for, Mr. Seager?"

"Just general notes, nothing like an exact record," Seager said. "I have several of these—what—disputes, friction problems, you understand, and it may be a while before we can give them our attention. Just a note here and there to remind me, a rough outline."

"Yes. I have the utmost respect for Rusty Bracken," Merryweather said. "The best, the very best. On the Board, but he hasn't lost touch with the realities of selling. The company couldn't function without him, he doesn't mind rolling up his shirt-sleeves. A beautiful wife, two lovely kids. He showed me photos of them once. A nice Persian cat."

"Suppose they made that new rule in the blue-book," Grayson said.

"Everybody is to call him Mr. Bracken, according to the rule. He wouldn't stand for it."

"Well, of course an exception could be made in his case."

"Well then, an exception could also be made in your case, Harry. If we have exceptions, Harry, we have exceptions. Harry."

Seager said: "Ah, the coffee-cart. My goodness, 10.30

already. Good morning, Miss Janizcowski. No sugar. Thank you."

"Regular, please, Christa," said Merryweather.

"Thanks, Booties," Grayson said.

"Now, gentlemen, here's my own view about this," Seager said. "Mr. Merryweather, unfortunately it doesn't seem to me that there's sufficient distance between your grading and Mr. Grayson's to justify company intervention, a company disciplinary instruction to Mr. Grayson. I sympathize with your grievance—as I say, the implications do favour you, but imagine the precedent we'd establish by making a decision on such a close basis. Floods of similar complaints, my hands full, no, these borderline matters are best left flexible. Mr. Grayson, may I say that I seriously deplore your attitude, both to Mr. Merryweather and to the company itself. I find your attitude frivolous and argumentative."

"But what about the precedents we have already?" Merryweather said. "What about the people George addresses as *Mr.* who have the same seniority or less?"

"Well, that would be the flexibility I mentioned. The personal adjustments, and I suppose these tolerances are regrettable if one takes the view that—"

"But if I can't have, why don't you make a rule that the others can't too? That'd be just as good. Every bit as good."

"It's the same argument, Mr. Merryweather."

"No, it isn't. The first says junior grades *must* address those senior grades with a certain respect . . . and God *knows* I can't understand why . . . why . . . the second, it's entirely different, the second says that these senior grades *needn't*, *shouldn't* be addressed, all of them, no exceptions . . . . Oh."

"Effectively the same argument. Sorry, Mr. Merryweather. What's wrong?"

" . . . different, entirely different . . . *please*. Oh, I can't help myself. Oh. Oh."

"Are you ill, Mr. Merryweather?"

"What's the matter, Harry? Pull yourself together, man."

"It's *always the same*. Nothing I do comes out right, ever.

Nobody . . . will talk to me at parties. When I join a group. They break up and join other groups. When I stand alone . . . on my own, by myself, standing and smiling, pretending to be happy . . . waiting . . . hardly anybody comes near me. And I'm never successful with *women*, and I *was* never, ever successful with *girls*, when . . . . They don't understand my jokes, they stare at my *tie* when I make one, and the women I *get* now and then . . . not often, now and then . . . they're always looking for *something else*, a house, a marriage, a dinner. My wife married me to be married, after she'd finished enjoying her . . . when it was time for her to marry, after. . . . Oh, she hates me. She only *makes love* to me twice a month. When *she* wants to, for *health reasons*. I have a boy . . . a son, fourteen . . . and he can't bear to live in the same house with me. Philip. I'm always offering to take him on fishing trips, but he sneaks off on fishing trips alone. He isn't rebelling against authority . . . he's rebelling against *me*. The dog tries to bite me every night when I come home. My mother . . . oh God . . . she preferred her stepson to me, Dietrich Jonas the Saskatoon strangler, eleven dead. . . . She *preferred* him, a good boy, just the bad company, but look at *you*, what are you? They're always promoting people past me, they never stop it. . . . Everything is *moving*, while I just . . . I've made four grades in fifteen years, and I'm the hardest worker in the Division. I stay till seven, I carry a full briefcase. . . . Mr. Bassett, a Kleenex oh where oh thanks he sends me *memos* rather than talk to me. I make him shiver. He hasn't spoken more than four words to me in seven weeks now. He came to the company as a messenger six years ago. We called him Alf. I use three cans of spray deodorant a week."

" . . . rest of the day off, Mr. Merryweather," Seager said. "Perhaps stay in bed tomorrow too, and call your doctor. You're extremely upset."

"Big baby. He's a big baby. He's a big cry-baby, that's what."

"Look. See this key-ring? Ten keys. *Ten*. Do you know how many I use? Two. One of the others, this one here, was for an old suitcase, I threw it away years ago. And this one was for a tape-recorder I used to own. Just a thing to play with in the evenings. I sold that to buy my wife's engagement ring at Birks. See, it's old, how worn it is. . . . I've forgotten what the others were. I've been carrying. These useless keys around for years, years . . . putting them on the bedside table with my change and spectacles, you understand. Oh what's the use, what's the use of talking, I mean *jingling* them in my pocket, the good solid bunch, searching in them for my. Front door key every night, because a man should have a hefty bunch of *keys*. Who can respect a man with only *two keys*? What? I need protection! My position is threatened! An important man has plenty of keys oh God yes, and he has. A thick wallet with lots of identification. From private credit companies, not just the Transport Minister of Ontario."

"Well, it isn't my fault, is it?" said Grayson. "I mean, all of us have our own problems, haven't we? What's the point of crying in an office? I can give you another Kleenex but that's about it."

"Mr. Merryweather. I'd like you to take my advice. Call your doctor. Get a prescription for meprobamate."

"Advice is cheap, and so is Kleenex by God. You two don't know. What does anybody know about the toll it takes? I'll tell you something else."

"There, there. Hush now."

"Listen to him go. A grown man. Isn't this unusual?"

"No, in fact."

"I'm surprised at that."

"We have a lot of weeping in here from day to day. We have these desks that can be wiped dry. By all means feel free to leave now, Mr. Grayson. I've kept you from your office long enough."

"But I mean I do understand the man. I understand the poor fellow, and I can't leave him in this state. The argument, I mean, isn't worth all this. He's had it tough."

"The dispute has certainly cost the company money, Mr. Grayson. I'm blaming you for provoking and prolonging it. I'd like to get at some letters now."

Merryweather said: "I'll tell you something else. I went to my wife's church, RC because I had to change. I bought a missal, the RC prayer-book for following the mass. My wife wanted me at church every Sunday, but when she saw I was interested—just as soon as she noticed me following the mass, *she* stopped going. She stopped going to mass, snap, that's how much it meant to her. Though I had to change, I took three months of special instruction, twice a week, Tuesdays, Thursdays. Memorizing a catechism, and getting it right about where the saints stood, and plaster images. She said there were too many Italians in the local church, the garlic got in her clothes she said, and snap. That parish priest was intelligent for an RC, he had the answers, and he was built like a wrestler, a wrestler with a bald head and a thick neck, shoulders, short legs, you know how they are. . . . Like walking with tree stumps, and then the arms hooked out. So because he acted so confident and everything I thought there might be, you know, a God or something. With this huge priest at a high mass, I was kneeling there as usual when he turned to the people, the voice like a bull's, this huge priest oh my God, before they dropped the Latin, a bellow, CREDO IN UNUM DEUM, I believe in one God, it nearly killed me. I'd never heard such a shout of happiness, it went through my stomach and my brain, it nearly killed me. I had to grab the seat I was shaking so much, I held on. Not a measly *prayer*, nothing *holy* or anything the way he said it. A bellow of happiness, that was it, just bursting out, he had it. I knew he was right. We were crawling around in the dirt, and he. . . . He was a man with a *God* to answer to. I got caught on the *savage* part, the body and the voice, *savage joy*, that was what came out of his lungs, and I swear I looked up and saw the man's God, oh I saw the power, bigger than all the distance of space. Farther away than the *stars*, farther away than we can ever see or ever know, and better, better than—"

"Mr. Merryweather," Seager said. "Mr. Merryweather, would you remember that we're in a place of business? We're sensitive as a company to the human element, but still. We're a profit-making concern, primarily. This is an office. Ask your doctor for the 400 mg. meprobamate and take two."

"Let him finish, why can't you? Let the poor bastard

spill it out, if that's what his present need is. I didn't know any of this. I'm interested in all this stuff."

"I saw the face of God."

"Please stop now. It's embarrassing."

"Go on, Harry. Go on, let her come. We're with you."

"Of course, I'm not stupid, I knew it wouldn't last. There was too much happiness, far too much—*happiness*. I only wanted to keep some of it, a bit. The next week was the week I remember because it stayed. I hardly noticed at first when the slipping started, everything happened so slowly, changing so slowly I didn't notice, like growing older. I didn't *feel* anything draining away, but it did. So I lost all of it. I lost the thing I got, and I lost the first thing of my own, that was gone too. Everything just trickled away, like the sink-water when the girl pours in a capful of Ease-Flo, the Magic Drain Cleaner, slowly. As they say, an Ease-Flo chore the more you pour, down it goes lower and lower."

"Well, what happened?" said Grayson.

"I have appointments for the afternoon," Seager said. "Letters I'd like to get at. You gentlemen are in my office."

"What do you *think* happened? What have I been talking about? Nothing happened. I was empty, and then nothing else happened. Nothing's happened since. I had a cuspid cavity filled last March. I won $4.75 in a mail lottery. My wife goes to the church bingos and she doesn't complain about garlic. I bought a .22 rifle for my son's birthday and he won't let me try it out. I've got a TV in my own room and a teapot and I shut the door. I take in salty chips, Niblets."

"Harry, who knows about this God stuff?" Grayson said. "It seems to me we're wide open on it. We're still wide open on the big ones. We're pretty ignorant as we stand. We don't control anything much that's happening, do we?"

"I have both of your files here," Seager said. "Yours and yours. I see there are excellent reports on the quality of your work, both very high, a top rating in fact. Now, before anything is done to set you back, or spoil the record, would you agree now to forget this little fight? Just to drop it. Let it be, or work out some private accommodation, I don't care personally. Would you agree at this stage? We've had a good talk."

"I didn't know about reports being done on work," Grayson said. "What reports? Is it some spy system or what? I didn't know about that. I'm interested in that. How often do you do them?"

"*Who's* been doing excellent reports on my work?" Merryweather said. "Mr. Seager, this is . . . very good news. Excellent reports. Why didn't somebody tell me? Excellent reports, and I thought . . . I believed everybody hated me. Who wrote the reports? Mr. Bassett? Did Mr. Bassett write excellent reports on my work?"

"These files are confidential. Don't push."

Grayson said: "Well, if he's got such excellent reports, why hasn't he been promoted? He has a raw deal. Four grades in fifteen years, I mean. How come?"

"Company promotion policy is confidential, of course. What's more, your question, Mr. Grayson, is pushy. I don't wish to lose my temper."

"Oh, come on now, Ted, get off the company high horse. We eat in the same cafeteria on Wednesdays."

"What?"

"The man's career is all he has. His whole life, even. Why don't you give him the annual grade, what's the problem if his work is so good?"

"What did you call me just now?"

"How's that?"

"What did you call me just now?"

"Call you? I didn't call you anything."

"You called me Ted."

"Well, certainly I called you Ted. It's your name. What else should I call you?"

"Call me Mr. Seager, please, *if* you please, Mr. Grayson. The same courtesy I pay to you."

"I meant to ask you about that. That Mr. Grayson, Mr. Merryweather business of yours, because I don't get it. I mean, this isn't even an English firm. I don't get it. We're Canadian. You can call me George. Let's all loosen up."

"I have no desire to call you George. We're not English,

but neither are we American and the courtesies are important, Mr. Grayson. You're new, of course, and I'm making all allowances—"

"I'm new here, sure, yes, but I'm not new in the business. I've been in places where the company prexy—"

"It isn't our practice here. We like to give honour where honour is due. In my own case, the relationship is a formal one with staff. Quite apart from the matter of grading."

"Oh, tish. I know the blue-book section on grades. A personnel director but not a Vice-President, I'd say you were about M2, depending on seniority, not really very far above Harry here. What I don't like is the way you ride the company high horse. I didn't know about the spy-system either."

"As it happens, my seniority, fifteen years, puts me—"

"Harry's got fifteen years."

Merryweather said: "This is a silly argument."

"My chief powers," Seager said, "are outside divisional policy, because I'm empowered to act in personnel matters affecting staff up to the D level. I have powers of dismissal, for instance, up to three grades above your present one, Mr. Grayson."

"Well, you'd have some explaining to do. I'm an extremely rare cog. I'm in demand. They had trouble getting me. They started me with a five thousand raise and the two thousand maximum expense fringe. It'll be in that file somewhere. Mr. Rookes wants me to sign a contract and I'm holding out."

"This office is responsible to the Board, not to divisions, departments or individuals. The Board has never queried a decision from this office. Never."

"Use your head, Ted," said Grayson. "You're fretting."

"George is right, Mr. Seager," said Merryweather. "George is right, Ted. We're wasting company time. I don't want to know why I haven't been promoted. I'm not curious. I'm honestly not curious."

"I'll submit a report of our conversation to Mr. Rookes."

"Mr. Rookes likes me. He's asked me to dinner. His wife thinks I'm outdoorsy."

"But Mr. Rookes doesn't like Mr. Merryweather, does he Mr. Grayson? I can act. I can act on Mr. Merryweather and no argument. How would that strike you, Mr. Grayson? You'd be the troublemaker responsible. How would that sit on this tender conscience of yours?"

"Why would you do that?"

"He just called me Ted. The rot is spreading out from you. He's been talking about God and his love life. I have letters to get out."

"Well, I guess I'd support Mr. Merryweather. I'd follow through."

"What you mean to say is that you'd support Harry. Isn't that it? You'd support Harry. Harry."

"No. I mean I'd support Mr. Merryweather. I'll give him the Mr. Merryweather now. I didn't know about this God stuff. I just based my prejudice on one or two details. Just *Fugitive Bride* and the jokes."

"But you don't like him."

"Sure I like him."

"Do you really, George?"

"Certainly I do, Mr. Merryweather. You're tops in my book."

Seager said: "Mr. Grayson, I believe that you're frivolous all through. You didn't like Mr. Merryweather when you came into this office."

"I like him now. I like Mr. Merryweather pretty well now."

"Why?"

"Why not? A man can change his mind."

"Not a good businessman with firm judgment."

"A businessman is still a man. You make a businessman sound like a Martian. He's a human being."

"Ah, but there's exactly where you're wrong. There's your error. A good businessman operates under special conditions, like a good soldier in war. A soldier would lose battles if he kept remembering that he was a human being."

"I don't like what you call the implications of that. What are you implying—the human ethic goes out the window?"

"That's war or business, isn't it? The priorities are

different. If I get a job applicant who needs the job desperately—wife sick, children hungry—I can't let the circumstances influence my decision. Oh yes, I feel properly sorry, naturally—as a human being if you like—but as a good businessman I must pick the right man for the company. If I staffed this place with deserving cases we'd soon be out of business. Business is business. All those precious human feelings are weapons or weaknesses. Compassion weakens a man, and love, love is a weapon, too, and so is fear. Everybody knows this."

"Fear, yes, I can see that. I can see fear," Grayson said.

"He's right about love as well, George," said Merryweather. "Sorry, I mean Mr. Grayson. Love is a weapon. They'll use it against you if they have it, in the office or out of it. They'll beat you with love on the head like a club."

"A good businessman keeps his defences up," said Seager.

"No need for the *Mr.* for me, Mr. Merryweather," said Grayson. "Go right ahead and call me George. I'm not a good businessman by these standards. I'm surprised I got this far, with the situation as you define it. I'll go ahead and call you Mr. Merryweather now, and you call me George."

"I'll call you George, then. But you must call me Harry."

"I don't mind. If it means something to you I'll call you Mr. Merryweather. No skin off my nose, to tell the truth."

"I think, seriously, I'd prefer you to call me Harry, George. I *feel* it, the thing is I'm grateful to you."

"But that doesn't help you in this business sense, though, does it, Harry? I know. I know what I can do. I'll call Mr. Rookes Mike and I'll call Mr. Watson Jim. I'll start this afternoon. They can't do a thing about it. How would that appeal to you?"

"That's very good of you. I'd like that. Thank you."

"I'll start this afternoon. Mike and Jim."

Seager said: "God. This is a deteriorating situation. Look. Let me quote you an example. Last week a woman came here applying for cost-bookkeeper K4 to 6. She'd just left hospital. A car accident, killed her husband and two children. She was driving, so her confidence was gone she stated. Before the accident she was a fashion model at $40 an hour, hardly ever out of work. She wept on that desk—real wet tears. I wiped them off with this chamois, look, I keep it here in the second drawer. The desk wipes dry. I could see more of her confidence going. Just imagine the blow to her. She couldn't even get a job as a cost-bookkeeper, she was rejected for a K grade."

"That's not too interesting, that stuff," Grayson said. "I mean, it doesn't illuminate any principle. All it shows is that you hang tough in this office. I already knew about stern behaviour. Making women cry and wiping the desk off."

"Hasn't our disagreement been settled now?" Merryweather said. "George?"

"Yes, we're clear here," Grayson said. "Well, thanks for your time, Ted. Or Mr. Seager, whichever makes you feel loosest. Thanks for helping us straighten it out. I guess we'll let you get started on those letters. You could probably crank out five before lunch."

"Thanks a lot, Mr. Seager," Merryweather said. "I appreciate this. I appreciate you letting me know about those excellent reports, incidentally."

"We're not straightened out, we're balled up," Seager said. "There's a principle illuminated OK, and you've missed it. I wasn't just hanging tough when I turned the girl away. I was *doing my job well*. See? We were looking for an efficient cost-bookkeeper. My job was to fill the vacancy for a cost-bookkeeper. And I did it. There's a good cost-bookkeeper in that vacancy now, and not some fashion model getting rehabilitated at company expense. We're not a *hospital*."

"Well, I suppose you have these things in your department," said Grayson. "I guess we all like to talk shop, if we can find somebody who'll listen. Personally I'd like to trot back to my desk now. Nobody's standing in for me, and the paper keeps on coming."

"But can't you see I was doing my job?"

"Mr. Merryweather probably wants to get away too. We're in your office. This won't buy the baby new shoes, eh Harry?"

"I'm all behind," Merryweather said. "I'm all behind like an elephant. Get it? All behind, like an elephant."

"I get it right enough," Grayson said. "This may be a little harder for me than I thought."

"It won't do. Your solution is rotten. Sit down, please. Sit down, Mr. Merryweather. Sit down, Mr. Grayson. We haven't finished."

"I don't have to listen to your personnel-department problems, you know. My responsibility is of a different kind. I don't have to listen to that story about the fashion model."

"Well, listen to this one. What'll happen when you start Mikeing Mr. Rookes and Jimming Mr. Watson? I'll be sitting in this chair again tomorrow morning. I can't take a whole lot of it. I'm not supposed to be on it full time. Mr. Rookes is marginal, but one Jim to Mr. Watson from you and he'll be standing on that carpet in his desert boots."

"Right," Grayson said. "Go ahead. I'll listen a little."

"If we had the rules, as I suggested," said Merryweather, "your time wouldn't be invaded in this way, Mr. Seager. See how simple everything could be? We're relying on people making *concessions*."

Seager said: "I was looking for a cost-bookkeeper. I wasn't looking for a distressed fashion model. My weaker part said give her the job. As a businessman I turned her down. Mr. Grayson, do you understand that?"

"Perhaps she'd have made a good cost-bookkeeper?"

"Not a chance. You have to understand P&L accounts and trial balance. I showed her a slide-rule and she guessed it was for drawing parallel lines."

"Well, you *can* use a—"

"I'm admitting—so far as I can tell, I'm not a doctor—that the job would have helped her."

"A fashion model would definitely liven up that costing department. That department is dead. They sit in there like sitting mummies."

"The department is efficient. We don't want her lively."

"I'm not happy about the idea of depending on personal *favours*." Merryweather said. "I shouldn't have to feel grateful, should I? If I'm entitled to the respect, why should I have to feel grateful?"

"A fashion model in cost accounting," Grayson said. "Where's your imagination, Ted? A long-legged model on the parquet runway between the comptometers. Getting the eye from all the bifocals. Then catching the ancient sly eye of HM himself, his majesty the prexy, because he spends enough time in there checking us out. Then she becomes his mistress. Then he divorces his wife, Ethel. Then he hasn't those frustrations of a morning. Then he doesn't need to hear Ethel's instructions of an evening on how to run the company, based on female intuition and malice. Then he takes to buying a few roses now and then. Then he tells the laundry to put less starch in his shirts. Then he learns a song or two for the bathroom, and stops wearing the nine-button waistcoat."

"Then he isn't as good a businessman."

"Human beings can be good businessmen."

"No."

"I know some human beings who are good businessmen," said Merryweather. "Not far from where we're sitting. Fine men."

"Possibly. But," said Seager, "those wouldn't be the real businessmen. Their defences would have holes. A good businessman keeps his defences up."

Grayson said: "He could well be right, you know, Harry. Look at it the other way: I can't think of any good businessmen who are human beings. The real ones, as he says."

"That's preposterous. There must be millions."

"I didn't say there weren't any. I said I can't think of any."

"What about me?" said Merryweather.

"Harry, I think you're a human being. I'll leave it there."

"Why am I not a good businessman?"

"Why haven't you been promoted?"

"Ask him. Not me. How should *I* know? That's what my life is full of, mysteries. What about yourself, may I ask, please?"

"I don't honestly know, Harry. It's a game we play.

The purpose of the game isn't the product, and it isn't the money we get for playing. We're supposed to enjoy the game itself, just playing along. That's as far as my understanding of the theory goes, anyway. Nobody's worked the theory out in detail. We're in the dark ages on this thing. We're filling in time. So that we don't have time to think about the time. Everybody must believe that next Tuesday will be better. The life we're waiting for is the only one we enjoy. You can pick up a lot of these ideas by reading poetry on the weekend, but they don't help. You can pick them up in the newspapers too, if you know what you're looking for. They don't help, though."

"What exactly do you mean, Mr. Grayson?" Seager said.

"Your defences are too far up," Grayson said. "Me and my weekend mouth. If I get a reputation for talking this way I'm dead, company-wise."

"Leftish, you mean?" Seager said. "I wouldn't worry. We're tolerant of all political views, as you know. But surely the company's place in a man's life is simple enough. It provides our existence, and we see that it continues to exist and grow. Take me. I have a wife and two children. I love them, of course, and they depend on me for food, shelter, education, a worthwhile place in the society. There's your motivation. You don't need poetry to figure it out. Of course I also enjoy my work. Though enjoying the work is no guaranteed part of the arrangement. I'm not enjoying myself this minute, but I'm doing it. I'm having a terrible time, but I'll lick her. If my work fails, my family suffers."

"Well, it's pretty tribal, as an opinion," Grayson said. "As a way of looking at the world. I understand the motive, it's the one that turns the wheels. Hard to argue with. But they keep telling us we're further along, that's all I'm saying. There's a general feeling in the air that we're further along. A bit of honesty shouldn't hurt. All this *Mr.* nonsense just hides the truth. We should be calling each other Pointed Fang and Manslayer."

"Oh, I hate people who won't grow up," said Seager. "They're so proud of their little sensitivities. Their faces shine and they're so smug and they're so superior. They're so ignorant, that's it. THEY-DON'T-KNOW-THEIR-ARSE-FROM-THEIR-ELBOW! What do you call a human being? What's so precious about them? WHERE ARE THEY? They come into this office with grievances. They weasel, they try to con me, they weep, they tell lies and they show no dignity. They act like children. How can I respect them? They flatter me, they carry tales, and then they go back to their desks and write me smooth memos. This is their way, flattering, backbiting, weaseling and lying, and where are the exceptions? What makes a human being valuable, as such? No, Mr. Grayson, I'm for the company. The company is hard, but it's clean. It's better than the people in it."

Merryweather said: "And a man needs it. Because it's bigger than he is, so naturally he wants to belong to it, that should be obvious. It stands out a mile. I have no left-wing sympathies myself. I've outgrown that stage, and now I'm true blue."

"Better and bigger?" Grayson said. "I guess so, if we decide to be midgets. Well, I might just dampen that desk if I start on the things a man could grow on. He could explore places, the Andes in Peru. He could learn how to read music or how to cure ailments. He could be a companion of the lonely, nine to five. He could drive a fire engine. He could search the world for love. He could grow fields of coleus. He could set slaves free. He could live near a river. He could give grins to children. He could practise hope, he could write letters with cheer in them, oh he could do a million things and grow. Instead he lines up for the ferris wheel and never gets off. Do you even understand how your TV set works, Harry? What makes the pictures?"

"It's the frivolousness again," Seager said. "I can speak from experience on this. It'll ruin you."

"No."

"You're not the first. I get reams of this same attitude, and they all think it's individual."

"No. Cowardice, that's what's ruining me, Ted, if you want to know, just ordinary cowardice. I'm being ruined by a lack of plain bravery. A lack of guts. Weakness and fear, awful twins. Too much love of trifles, like Scotch whisky and good food and tailored clothes and carpeted rooms. I haven't enough of the important qualities, not in the little cells of my body. I can respect you, Ted, even though I can't respect your beliefs. I want to throw up when I look at myself, and at people like Harry here."

"Me?" said Merryweather. "Me?"

"Oh, face it, Harry, for Pete's sake. You'll never make it in this company."

"Who said I'll never make it? Who the hell do you think you are, you snooty bastard?"

"Face facts," said Grayson. "Acknowledge the facts, when they're hard up against your eyeballs."

"I don't like your tone, George. The tone of voice when you say my name, when you say Harry. You've been allowed a privilege and you're abusing it."

"Never mind. I apologize."

"See, you're putting yourself on the same level. He's putting himself on the same level again. He's abusing the privilege."

"Mr. Merryweather," said Seager.

"What privilege?" said Grayson.

"This is promising talk," Seager said. "Good, go on."

"I'll never make it, won't I? What gives you the right to say that? Walking around here, in a business office, your head stuffed with nonsense, and telling me I'll never make it. I can call the TV repairman if the picture goes, can't I? That's his *job*, fixing the picture. We'd better return to the earlier arrangement."

"And that was?" said Seager. "Which arrangement?"

"He calls me Mr. Merryweather and I call him George. I shouldn't have allowed him the privilege, because now he's abusing it."

Grayson said: "We never got that arrangement arranged, Harry. You're a *mole*."

"Well, time we did, you snooty bastard."

"Hold on a minute," Seager said. "This is better. Mr. Grayson, may I understand that you won't then be calling Mr. Rookes Mike and you won't be calling Mr. Watson Jim?"

"I won't. Not so's this one can stay blind. Look at him. A gift so rare that we can't understand it, an interruption of oblivion. We're flinging it away as if we had a thousand years. He's a mole. He's Harry, that's who he is, Harry the mole."

"Good," Seager said. "Let's make another effort. Would either of you consider a transfer to one of the branches? Let's start there. Mr. Grayson?"

BROTHER AND SISTER

Jane Rule

"My father is bigger than your father," the sister said.

The brother looked to middle space, vaguely enraged, his eleventh shot of vodka on an octagonal table the size of a dinner plate, set next to the large chair he was occupying. It occurred to him that this might be his sister's chair, though she was sitting across from him in something very upright and insubstantial.

"My chair is bigger than your chair," he tried, not convinced he had the hang of whatever game she was playing.

She took a sip of Coca Cola from a bottle and put it down on a carved chest, pimpled with coasters, small ash trays, lighters and painted stones. He took the same sort of sip from his shot glass, lips embracing it; and, when he had swallowed, he left the glass in his mouth and stuck his tongue out into it. She didn't look at him, leaving him to enjoy himself or not. The light was very bright beyond her. He could neither hold the pose nor watch her for long; so he took the glass out, leaned over the arm of the chair and very carefully dropped the glass to the floor, watching as if rings might form and travel over the carpet. She turned at the sound, got up, picked up the glass and walked out of the room.

Having scored, he dozed for a moment, then woke generous with victory, if a little confused about it. They ought to go fishing. They always had a good time fishing. She didn't ever fish. She carried the lunch and sat on various rocks and didn't say anything at all. He admired himself in her eyes when she was like that. He cast and could see himself casting, a big man with a beautiful, accurate wrist.

"Are we going fishing some time?" he called out, but there was a machine on somewhere. "It's like a goddamned factory," he said and tried getting up to complain.

He didn't have trouble walking, for all the threat of little objects. Not exactly a cluttered room, just unexpected things, like that dinner-plate table and those painted rocks. There was one of them in front of him now, probably a door-stopper got loose from somewhere, travelling around the house on its own like a turtle. He'd have to be careful until he learned his way around, knew what he might meet, in light or dark.

By the time he found the kitchen, he had forgotten his negative intent. There was the vodka bottle for one thing and his sister for the other, standing with her back to him, staring down at whatever she was grinding up in the sink. He leaned against the refrigerator, had a long blink, deciding against either fart or belch, opened his eyes and yawned instead. Somewhere in the middle of it, she snapped a switch. The silence quite sobered him.

"I'm getting drunk," he said. The statement didn't require an answer, and he got none; so he went to the bottle and helped himself. "Good and drunk."

"I'll feed you in a few minutes."

"Sounds like the zoo," he said. "Feeding time at the zoo. You know, you've got to watch those turtles. They can be a real hazard to traffic around here. Guy could break his damned leg on one of them."

She had gone to the stove. Women's backs always looked offended, clothed or not. Never could see the erotic in a woman's back. Always offended.

"It's a nice place," he said. "I like it. I'm not mad about the turtles, I admit, but that's a matter of taste."

"And the snakes and the flying paper clips and the owl with elephantiasis," she said agreeably. "It gets crowded."

"Well, we're big people, with big imaginations," he said. "Some things you learn to put up with."

"I suppose."

"We've got the same father," he said then, testing.

"Maybe."

"Only I belittle him and you believe in him. There's no genetic argument. Our mother is a virtuous woman, in that narrow sense. Wouldn't you say so?"

"I'd say so."

"Good. Now, when are we going fishing?"

"Fishing?"

"Never mind," he said. "As long as we agree."

"You have to eat and then sleep for a while. There are all these people coming in tonight."

"People?" There was something menacingly bland about her face as she turned to him. "Baby, what do we need with people? I've got all these lousy stories to tell you, and we can fight about all our relatives and talk about our post-Freudian childhood." Her expression hadn't changed. "Well, sure, people. Why not? We'll go fishing some other time. Another trip. Or come on up to Alaska with me now, why not?"

She was saying no in an elaborately long sentence, maybe more than one. He lost control of other people's speech long before he lost control of his own. And then she was talking about people, back at the stove again. He yawned once more until the tears came, but his head didn't quite clear. He got the people and the mushrooms in the pan connected, walked over and had a good look.

"This one's with Fink Brothers?" he asked for verification. "And what did you say to remember? The wife's mother is . . . ?"

"A trustee," she answered.

"Some people have all the bad luck. You'd better feed me."

She didn't wake him. A sharp, brief pain, as specifically located as a crack in the ice, brought him down into the sound of people in another room. He felt disagreeable but required. She had unpacked his suitcase, which was nice of her, though it made the whole process of dressing very difficult. Seeing his suit in the strange closet was no more friendly an experience than finding his face in the mirror, in living colour without knobs to adjust. "And this is my Uncle Bill . . . by marriage. Poor, old Aunt Sarah." She couldn't get away with that. They were blood kin all right, past the blood in his eyes and his neck, nerve and bone kin. Bitch! bitched. "I'm bigger than your father," he tried, and that cheered him up for a moment because the suit was the right size, and except for that face—too bad he couldn't unscrew it and replace it with an extra from his suitcase, something freshly cleaned and not too wrinkled—he was grossly impressive.

Perhaps he could get to a drink before he had to encounter anyone. He had stupidly given her all the liquor he'd brought with him. He tried to remember the geography of the house, a big house for someone who mostly lived alone. He might get down and out the front door, then around to the back and into the kitchen, but it was unlikely. He looked at his watch. It was eleven o'clock. Had she hoped finally he wouldn't wake up? Easier the embarrassment of his absence than his presence? She wasn't like that. She didn't care. His sister.

In gold, a lighter shade but the same colour as her Greek honey hair, which was a lighter shade but the same colour as her Greek honey eyes. The man she was talking to looked beyond her through thick lenses and said something out of the side of his mouth, an animated cartoon.

"Mr. Magoo, come to life," the brother said, approaching the offered hand with what he considered to be a gentle smile.

The hand his sister tried to lay on him he took and kept for the whole circle of the room, as if instead they were children crossing a wide street. He wanted to look protective, though both of them knew that she was the one who wasn't afraid of dogs or cars. The room was full of both, women with low, barking voices, men peering through the windshields of their executive wooden frames, heavy and black this season.

"Alaska, yes," he said and adjusted his ear to the floor trying to pick out the female noise far below him. It was easier to keep talking. "Yes, about our father's business— that vast, vulgar, meretricious what's-it."

She pulled him along.

"I'm having trouble with my contacts," he said, bare and bleeding-eyed, but more comfortable at their nearly mutual altitude, which gave them a sort of privacy wherever they were. "Shall I have a drink?"

"Why not?" she said.

There was a puppet behind the bar, a ridge of plastic hair painted black, eyes that closed when his head went too far back, voice of a queer batman in a World-War-Two movie. "Yes sir."

"No sir," the brother said, no human help there, and he wanted to accuse his sister as he prepared to abuse himself.

"Who's the crow-footed adolescent?" he asked.

"That's the mother. . . . "

"Trustee," he said, but of what he couldn't think.

He couldn't tell whether he had cast her off or had been cast off. He made his slow, enormous way across the room and sat down on the floor at the trustee's feet, watching first her shoes, then the controlled varicose veins in her legs, the bony awning of her lap, and skipped, in a failure of courage, to the crow's-feet of her face. What was it he was supposed to remember? Had he been warned or required or simply entertained by details? Her flattered mouth, lipstick travelling up away from it in fine lines, smiled at him. He blinked for relief and then smiled back.

"We're both victims of the red spider," he said, knowing he must resist any temptation to explain, but of course she asked him. "An African god who sold his mother-in-law and children to Sky for just a couple of bits of technical information. You know, mother-in-law jokes aren't really funny. For example. . . ."

She didn't laugh at the end of it, dutifully.

"But there's a real joke about a son-in-law," he said. "Which one *is* your son-in-law?"

She nodded across to Mr. Magoo, his mouth drawn in fast square and round shapes, slipping from side to side in his face.

"Ah, Mr. Magoo," he said and he didn't notice, studying his new subject, that she had stopped listening to him and was engaged instead, on her own level, with a younger, harder version of herself.

"I haven't made a good impression," he said to her varicose veins, got up and went back to the bar.

Several men had gathered there and opened their conversation to him at once with a deference that came from respect for his size or his relative or both. He was feeling better, more affable, as if he had somehow followed instructions to the end of them and was now free.

"Don't know a goddamned thing about refrigeration plants or television or plasser mining," he was saying. "One thing, and only one thing...." Dramatic pause while he tried to and did remember what it was. "I'm a guy who knows how many beans it takes to make five."

How long she'd been standing by him he didn't know. When he saw her, he handed her his glass. Turning back to his audience, he found they were gone. She was too, and he was alone by the bar, waiting for the puppet who was in no hurry to give him another drink.

Then he couldn't find all those people, the crow-footed adolescent, Mr. Magoo; they seemed to have gone some place in the house that he didn't know. He started down to the basement, but it was dark and quiet there. In the hall again, he could hear his sister's voice, a calling voice, and he went to find her at the open front door, a hand raised to the last guest on his way down the path.

"What the hell time is it?" he asked.

"Two-thirty," she said, walking past him to the kitchen where the puppet waited in a change of costume, his palm held up and out by an invisible string.

He went to where the bar had been and found it gone as well. It was unnerving.

"Sister!" he called. "Sister!" There she was, honey coloured still. "Christ! I thought maybe your stage had turned into a pumpkin, too. Is this whole place portable? Where can I get a drink?"

"In Alaska," she said.

"I'm not going to Alaska," he said.

"Aren't you?"

"No!" he shouted. "And you know goddamned well I'm not. I'm going to bed. Get me a drink."

She didn't hesitate so much as pause with that same

bland danger in her face. "Mr. Magoo has the impression that you drink too much."

"A very perceptive fellow," the brother said generously. "Sounds like a perspective employer."

"He was."

"I thought you had a job."

"I do."

"Baby, get me a drink, and then I'll listen to all your troubles."

"When am I going to listen to yours?"

"Any time," he said. "Any time at all. Let me tell you about this WCTU sister I've got, for one thing."

But once she had given him the bottle of vodka, he became aware of the effect of his badly-interrupted sleep.

"These parties in the middle of the night . . . I don't see how you take it."

He always woke very early. He was glad to see a last drink in the bottle. He took it carefully, not to shock his gut into revolt, and then waited to measure the little good it would do. There was something unpleasant, like disappointment, just below the pain in his head, which was sending its own messages. There had been some sort of party he'd got out of bed for. Had his sister been unhappy about something? It was none of his business, a head full of griefs of his own, which he had trouble enough keeping there out of her way. Alaska: "and he came out of the jungle rich, rich . . . " or whatever the hell it was. Was it today he had said he was going to Alaska? On the afternoon plane, that was it. The trouble was, you loved what you were related to. Accepting that, he tried to stay in bed a while, knowing she would get up as soon as she heard him; but a horizontal hangover wasn't to be endured for more than moments at a time. Once he was on his feet, he kept encountering objects. Wasn't that the chest of drawers from their grandmother's house? He thumbed the corner that had just bruised his side, knowing it for the corner that had scarred his head, at the hairline, during a game of blind man's buff. He hadn't known he was hurt until he heard her crying. Having considered and discarded various means of revenge, he went into the bathroom for a shower.

She knew about his breakfast: a glass of milk and a glass of orange juice with an egg in it; and he knew about her breakfast: silence with whatever else she decided on. A quiet woman anyway, except with machines and pots and pans. Odd that she didn't marry, really, being so quiet, being the colour of good whisky or honey, all that colour in the summer, carrying the memory of it in her eyes and hair on winter mornings like this one. She had her bad points. Quietness. In a conversation, what she had to say were just pieces broken off her silence, hard clues to it. You had to know her to know her. Sometimes he did. Sometimes he didn't. She might be irritated or sorry or nothing at all right now. That was unpleasant, disappointing. He looked at his watch to be sure an hour had passed since his first drink. He stood in the kitchen for his second.

"We could walk for an hour before you have to go," she said.

There was a hill to climb, a path that began wide enough for two to walk together, then narrowed for the first steep pitch, and, even though she knew the way, he went ahead because he always did, and he chose the place to stop as well, giving her breath as a gift from him. It was beginning to feel that way now. They climbed again, then stopped again, and then he went on alone, up toward the sky he had been sold to, which wasn't far away. At the top of the hill he looked back to see himself being seen by her, and she was there watching him, a big man against a near sky.

"I'm bigger than your father," he called to her, grateful.

But when he climbed back down to her, he saw that she was crying, and then he had to know how badly hurt he was, just for that moment, and to forgive her for it.

THE STORY OF A CAT

John Newlove

My friends, do I have a right to use your lives as if they too were only words? Once they were more but now the past is only verbal, plastic, ornamental, recitative according to an agreed code. I remember the code but now I do not always find it possible to recall the stories about myself, much less any anecdotes of your existence. I have to be reminded but I don't worry and this calmness will be the end of me. The cat is among the newspapers under the table.

Loneliness makes me extravagant, for me. It's hard to restrain invention when nothing else seems to exist, no matter how impoverished the discovery may be: in a desert men dream of water, not rubies. But, for myself, I had thought I was a sober person and perhaps I am since whatever extravagance I do display is only extravagant for me. To others it is always water passing and nothing more. The cat jumps onto my lap, back arched, plume stiff and high.

Don't send a mutant to do a man's job. People who know the rules but aren't adapted to them act awkwardly. Their manners are bent coat-hangers. Their lives stutter. Confident bewilderment shines inadvertently out of their twisting eyes. They can be trusted when they try to cheat you but beware their dangerous, complex and unpredictable honesties. The cat strolls along a windowsill, looking for flies.

Our only extravagance is me, so for God's sake give us some cash. Or I'll bite your feet. I have three chins to feed and I need silver buckles for my shoes. If I had shoes. I need empty champagne bottles to show the garbage man and dead oysters to stare at. At which to stare. I need to be able to fly to Oslo at a moment's notice, presuming I could get a seat on the flight from here to the local city. I need to be able to fly to Tasmania and wake up with my ears ringing in the best hotel in Tasmania and say to the immigrant Greek maid: "What's the name of this bloody place anyways? Eh? Are there many cats here?"

Everyone is always at the mercy of everyone else. Some years ago there was reported the story of a hotel employee in Zurich who had quarrelled with a porter and, to get some sort of revenge, had set fire to the building. Ten people died in the flames and cats too, no doubt.

I have always been nervous on airplanes and lately in cars as well, despite all the assurances and statistics. Reason seems to be no cure for fear. On one flight a passenger said of the pilot, "He wants to get there alive too." I said, "I know," but I was thinking that I wondered if the pilot did want to get there alive. Who could tell what aberrations might be about to manifest themselves in him, how his life was, what hotel porter or wife or stewardess or cat he might have quarrelled with just before the flight began?

But it's not simply in the matter of the burnt or ripped flesh that we all are at each other's mercy. As well there is simply the sudden bitter retort that wounds; the turning of a back; someone saying in a bored voice, "I know," to your great discovery: the joke gone sour because someone has decided to refuse to laugh; the hurting laughter that others will give, pretensions and ignorance humiliatingly exposed, catlike.

I won't speak of love or, even worse, of friendship, gone wrong, thrown away by one or another with some wilful act that cannot be recalled or apologized for or ever forgiven by the one to whom the harm is done or by the harmer. There must be moments in every life about which to tell the slightest portion of the truth would be too painful and too damaging. The cat is sad in the kitchen.

What a scuffling thing love is. The cat sits, idol-like, perfectly still, on the table.

There is a talent for uninterrupted interruption, which I seem to possess. I am a devotee of the boringly arcane, of deliberately unimportant events, of whole centuries during which absolutely nothing has happened, when not even a breeze blew and the cattle were quiet and immobile on the vast ranches for years at a time; when there was no time and men stood waiting for the first thought to appear. The cat slouches out of the room, into the hallway.

I am the sort of person who spends all his time waiting for the arrival of letters that have never been written. They will never be written; nor shall I be able to reply to what will not be said. No doubt the cat is on its haunches, around the corner.

There is always so much of the past, so much of the present, both spreading endlessly from side to side, the past crowded with shining animals, the present paved with sharp green glass grass, endless, endless. I wonder what the cat is doing?

What makes us think that we were to be individual?— or that we are? Our successful history is the history of ants, of the warrens of Mohenjo-daro, of the uniform faces of our enemies and the weakly different and undependable appearances of our friends. We are intelligent and a herd. Cats are stupid but we keep them to remind us of what we pretend to think true and admirable, trying to suppose that it is possible to be dependent and free in the same place.

Don't count on the prejudices of others being false, or your own being true. You may not always agree with yourself but you will continue to act as if you do, no matter which of the limited human masks you prefer to try to use to confuse those you meet and pass. By now the cat will be in the front room, drifting on.

The continually empty days of whisky talk vaguely to me. Was that a life I had? Was it? Mist, mist. One cat seemed to have walked into the bush to die. One walked out of the house into the city and never came back. One coughed softly and died staring. Another sits in a room twenty feet away.

Is it intention that is important or the ability to carry

out an intention? If I say I'll kill you and say it from the throat only, only from the voice-box, isn't it just as brutal as if I actually intended to do it but was unable to commit the act? Thoughtless utterance is a brutality in itself: one day the carelessly-said word may be taken with seriousness by some other person and acted on viciously. If I say I love you and don't love you but say it only to avoid difficulty, harassment, explanations, am I not being as brutal to both of us by lying, by not giving you a chance to understand (a chance that might result in love), by refusing to make the effort to understand and admit what it is that I love, what those things are and what their natures are that I desire? Desire sickens me. My first desire is hopeless; it can never be had. It is: Not to die. I don't know next whether to use the word think or the word feel, for I mean neither. There is an area that is of both and yet is neither. Perhaps I should use the word know, meant in an unprovable way. This unobtainability of my prime desire makes me know that all my other desires are unobtainable too. No. They are not unobtainable, as the first is: but they can never be satisfied. Thus, I wish to be loved and perhaps I am or have been loved. But I can never wholly believe it and even the most extravagant demonstrations quickly lose their power of conviction and must be replaced by other and more novel proofs, which in their turn fail, and on and on until the effort of the loving person to make me realize that she loves me disgusts me too; and then I wish to be free of it, to be gone away, still declaring my love but unwilling to accept any. This all leads to self-hatred. It's easier to blame oneself for every mistake than to attempt to understand anything. If I persecute myself I can be sure of a constancy: there will never be any embarrassingly sudden forgiveness for my acts from me. As a pursuer I am more merciless and more persistent than the Erinyes, and less just, and I will never leave myself alone. I will never be able to escape from my own revenge until I die. One cat was long and grey and quiet, never noticing when her kittens were killed season by season.

Not really feeling guilty, but afraid to be accused. The cat is in the room with me again, cheerful.

Rain: mizzle, drizzle, stillicidium. Thicker than a mist dropping on the downtown streets, quieting the dust, pushing aside the smoke from industry. Better to walk home slightly wet than breathing in the particles cars raise, teeth abrasive, roof of the mouth muddy, nose irritated, eyes sticky. But now it is almost nightfall: light shining by some prior arrangement through the cloud layers, through the tall tree, through the glowing yellow waxen blossoms of a bush in the front yard, falling onto the bright wet green grass. Drops of rain drip from the unnaturally clean leaves of the tree, through the top branches of which, growing almost straight up, thread the twin power lines. Electricity is seeping into my house against my will, costing me money I haven't got and won't have unless there is some minor sort of commercial miracle. A quiet millionaire falls anonymously, platonically, in love with me? Unexpected, unsigned letters with money orders for huge amounts, thus? An industrialist pities my bad teeth? He supplies two thousand, no, two-and-a-half thousand dollars in cash so my teeth can be fixed? Zoom, under general anaesthetic, a gentle and slow and dreamy zoom, mind you, and I wake up pristine, pearly, willing to smile again with my lips apart, shining whitely. And after the anaesthetic's vomiting, another nap, another awakening, the feeling of having had a long perfect shower that would clean me up once and forever and the knowledge finally comes upon me convincingly that I have nice teeth now, two-and-a-half thousand dollars tucked under my pillow, inside the pillow-case in a sealed manila envelope made doubly secure with magic mending tape. The languorously efficient nurse who will have been trying to think of some way to seduce me without messing up the sheets brings me the morning newspaper. It appears that the bottom has dropped out of everything in some way that I can't understand, but eggs are nothing for twelve dozen, cars are five dollars each, a fine house can be had for fifty or sixty dollars, everything is unbelievably cheap. The bill for fixing my teeth is $4.25 and I pay it with a five-dollar bill and tell the dental surgeon to keep the change. He simpers at me incredulously, he is the first Canadian dentist ever to have been tipped by a patient and he is sure that it would be unethical or at least undignified to keep the money, but I am rich and there is a complicated Japanese camera outfit he has been wanting so he can take colour slides of his goldfish. ... I stride out of the office, new-toothed and wealthy, $2495 in the manila envelope, re-taped with ordinary Scotch tape from the dentist's office. I pass a beggar in the street. Good God! It's the industrialist who gave me the money only a few days before! He whines for a handout, a penny, half a penny, a tenth of a penny, a *twentieth* of a penny, anything. He doesn't recognize me with my new teeth. But I have started to worry about having given the extra 75¢ to a dentist as a tip, because money doesn't last forever no matter how much you've got, the industrialist is an immediate example, and I'm also worrying about whether the languorously efficient nurse really would have wanted to seduce me or, if she did, if it would have been because she knew about my fortune. Can't trust strange women. And they're all strange. Money, money, that's all anyone cares about. Nobody loves me for myself. I pass by the industrialist, retired, pulling the sleeve of my shirt out of his humble clutch. I haven't anything smaller than a five anyways. I should buy a suit to put on over my shirt. I wonder if I should go back to the dentist's office, pretending that I never told him to keep the change, and ask for my 75¢ back? No. I haven't got the nerve. Mizzle, drizzle. It's still raining lazily and I still don't have any money. Never will have either. Never. Don't even know who sells the Irish Sweepstake tickets in this lousy northern town. Probably no-one. The loggers just play poker and I can't get into a game with no money. The cat sits on the table again. It rarely tires of playing idol.

The poison sea surrounds us. The poison sea surrounds us. The cat moves.

Is it more of a miracle to lose one's way stupidly and then to find it again through a chance at the last moment than to go straight to the mark from the very first? The cat is an idol again. Why doesn't it get tired?

Every man's death encourages me. Cats die by the

millions, before they have lived. Rats feast on them, breaking their bones for the marrow, building huge Aztec pyramids from the tiny skulls underground in their tunnels.

It died in one quick, solid burst of pain. The cat. Is that what eternity is?—that last hit, the last hurt, the last vicious cramping spasm of unendurable pain to be endured forever, the mind's lasting moment a scream of horror?

As for us, we have offered ourselves like sheep to the wolves. Why should we complain that the wolves, then, have become fond of mutton? The cat is gone.

A BAUBLE FOR BERNICE

Don Bailey

I woke up buzzing like a tuning fork. There was a constant humming in my head and body. Last night I arrived and drank the whole pint of rye from my tin cup. There was no water to mix with it but I wanted a celebration anyway. The bottle had been in my pack since I left Toronto, almost four thousand miles ago and I carried it through northern Ontario, across hot Manitoba and even in Saskatchewan when it began to rain, a rain that continued in Alberta and didn't let up until I was well into the Fraser canyon, and I never broke the seal and had one small shot to keep from getting a cold. Instead I got a cold that left me coughing for ten minutes when I got up this morning so that last night, arriving in Vancouver, I could celebrate. This morning I woke up with the closest thing to a hangover in three weeks.

The blue nylon tent had a film of moisture from my breath. I came awake actually startled. I had slept with a slight tension that even the whisky didn't completely wash away, a tension that someone would protest my tent being pitched on the beach so close to a residential area. I was sure a cop would shine his light in the doorway and yell at me to move on.

But I woke up alone and unmolested and I walked out on the beach spitting every ten feet. I was worried about the hard thing in my chest and I wondered if a doctor would take chargex. My cash was pretty low. I thought briefly about tomorrow, today really, when I would be on the train going back. I tried to think about going home.

In the ten years since I'd last been here, I'd forgotten about the ocean and its movement. I was surprised at the long stretches of wet sand that reached out 50 or 60 yards to the water's edge. The tide was out and I saw two women out near the water, one soft, bloated like the fish left by the water's sweep, and the other thin, neat and economical like the small sail-boats gliding around the bay; the women were dragging a huge canvas bag across the wet sand and appeared to be gathering something. I thought right away of clams and oysters because when I left Toronto I'd bought a fishing rod and had a plan to eat off the land. The only thing I'd ever caught was something a group of kids who were watching me haul them in from a riverbank in BC called squaw fish. Only the Indians ate them and even they choked. The flesh was mushy and they had too many bones.

I walked out farther and saw the women were picking up beer bottles that were half buried in the sand. The heavier one did the gathering and handed them to the slimmer girl, who shook the dirt from them and placed each one carefully in the bag. I was close enough to see that one of them had lighter-coloured hair than the other and I waved but they didn't notice me.

I walked back toward the tent. There was nothing there for me except that I should have taken it down and pulled out the sleeping bag to air, but I passed by, noticing that the tent had a bow in it from the wind and flapped dangerously like I imagined a sail on a small boat would and I was glad I was on land. I had never realized I was scared of water. I knew heights frightened me. I'd gotten a ride with one man all the way from Calgary and he'd taken me through the mountains in his little Japanese car that he kept saying, "holds the road tighter than your sister's cunt." What a sad awful man he'd been. When I mentioned all the rain he said it was good because up till then, "everything's been dryer than a nun's tit." I think he was a salesman. He didn't say much but he used a lot of words and he kept offering me menthol cigarettes because of my cough, but after five or six of them I only got hungry. He had nervous hands that were always fiddling with the radio, tuning in and out the static, pushing in the lighter, drumming on the steering-wheel that he hardly ever really hung on to, and every few miles he flipped on the wipers to scrape away the bugs who'd been killed against the speeding front window. He drove too fast but I couldn't say anything when he swerved around corners doing 70 when the signs had warned cars should slow to 40 or 50. Once in a tunnel through one of the mountain passes he honked at the car in front of us for going too slow and the brake lights of the other car flashed on, which must have scared him because then he slammed his brakes on and the wheels locked and we spun into the edge and dented the fender a little. He laughed and punched his fist into the palm of his other hand, but I thought we were pretty lucky there was no-one coming the other way. Probably we would have been killed but I never mentioned it. I smoked the rest of his menthol cigarettes even though I hated them, but he never slowed down until we got to the city limits.

"Gotta keep your eye open for radar," he said. "They got me around here three times."

I walked past the tent and up the hill where the houses were. One house had a window in front and one in back that were in direct line so I could see straight through. No-one appeared to block the tunnel effect, which in a way was too bad. I liked the people in that house. I liked the idea of living in a house with windows like that. It made me think of Bernice.

I was surprised when she asked for the divorce. We had everything.

"I don't understand," I said.

"Why should you? You hardly notice me anymore let alone understand."

"But I do." I did. She was always there. The apartment was untidy sometimes but she kept it clean and was always rearranging the furniture so I could hardly keep track of it, but that didn't matter. And she liked to make curtains and covers for cushions that made the place feel cheerful with all the different bright colours she used. Supper was rarely late and I told her all the time what a great cook she was. She was a perfect wife and I loved her.

"This isn't anything new," she said. "It's been going on for a long time and now I want out."

"What?" I said.

"This! This, you dummy." She was yelling and waving her arms around the room. She never talked like that.

"You wanna marry somebody else?" I said.

"No," she said and her voice sounded tired. "I want OUT, out. That's all."

"But why?"

And then her face got fierce like Cathy's does sometimes when I say something to her or ask her to do something. But Cathy is nine and Bernice is 30.

"I want a chance," she said, "to be alive. To be young. To do things!" And she was yelling again.

"What about Cathy?" I said. I knew that question would hurt her and for the first time in the ten years of our marriage I wanted to hit her, to really hurt her.

"She's yours, Rick."

I knew then that she'd made up her mind and I was going to lose unless somehow I could understand what was wrong with her.

"We could have a trial separation," I said.

"I want it to be over," she said. "It is, you know."

The whole thing was crazy. It happened so quickly I couldn't figure it out so it made sense. It was like a column of figures that I was trying to add up without my machine and the numbers kept slipping away on me so I'd have to start all over again.

"Bernice, I've gotta have time to think about this."

"I've thought about it," she said.

"Well I haven't!" and I yelled too.

She laughed.

"It's finished, Rick. What's the point?"

"I don't know what you're talking about. Maybe you need to see a doctor."

"For some pills," she said and she was still laughing. "Nice happy pills to make mommy happy."

"Have you talked to Cathy?" I asked.

"Yes and no."

"What's that supposed to mean?"

"I told her I wanted to make a life of my own, the same

way she'll want to make one of her own when she gets older."

"I'm sure that was crystal clear to her. A nine-year-old."

"You can talk to her yourself."

"Yes."

So finally we made an agreement. I would go away for a month and since school was out Cathy could come with me if she wanted to. I figured she would and Bernice could start the proceedings, whatever they were, and after a month I would come back and we would talk about it again.

I didn't have any trouble getting the time off from work. Next year I'll be senior bookkeeper and if I keep up my course I could be a CA in another two. I've been with the firm nine years and last year I only took a week's holidays because it was busy and I didn't want to be the guy to let them down.

Bernice sure fooled me the way she moved. She got a lawyer and had the papers drawn up charging me with adultery.

"Don't worry about it," she said. "It's just the fastest way to get it."

"But who's going to be . . . ?"

"Ruth said she would. All you have to do is say you did it with her to the lawyer and he gets you both to sign a paper and that's all."

So red-haired Ruth who lives across the hall and drinks coffee in the daytime with Bernice because she hasn't got anything to do but collect alimony cheques from her last husband, Ruth and I went to the lawyer's office and did what we were supposed to. It was easy but I didn't like the way the lawyer enjoyed himself saying intercourse more times than he had to.

A week later I still didn't know where I was going to go and I hadn't spoken to Cathy except to hint about a surprise. And then the lawyer called and Ruth and I had to go downtown and have the papers served on us. Ruth got all dressed up and I had to wait ten minutes for her to finish fiddling with her hair but it gave me a chance to notice she was really pretty. When we got there, a young girl smiled at us when I gave our names and whipped out a polaroid camera.

"Can ya stand a little closer together," she said smiling. And I could smell the perfume Ruth wore and felt her hip against me. The girl flashed the picture and suddenly I knew what I was going to do.

That afternoon I bought a 35mm camera. Before I got married I used to love to take pictures. And travel. I used to love to travel. Just wander around and if I saw something interesting, get it focused in the viewfinder and snap the shutter. That's what I was going to do, and I bought a small nylon tent, a rucksack, a fishing pole that folded up small, a sleeping bag big enough for two and finally a pint of whisky for when the journey was over. . . .

When I was 22 I'd hitch-hiked to Vancouver. Just before I got married. I did it for something to do and it gave me a chance to think about things. The idea of going back excited me for some reason. I didn't know anyone there and really it was just another place but maybe because of the ocean and the city being right at the edge of the country, some kind of a starting place, and I was satisfied not to understand why I was going there because the idea excited me, the idea of going back.

I don't know why I put off telling Cathy about my plan until the last moment. Bernice and I had talked it over, she thought Cathy was old enough to enjoy the trip and that probably she'd like it. But I kept putting it off until the day before I planned to leave. I woke her up early. It was a Saturday and Bernice was still sleeping.

"C'mon," I said. "I made breakfast. Bacon and eggs."

"OK," she grumbled. She's like Bernice, she likes to sleep.

I went back to make coffee and wait for her. She was a long time and still wore her flannel nightgown Bernice made. When I see her in the morning like that it makes me think of those shrubs or small trees that people wrap heavy paper around, to help the plant grow straight I guess. There's a certain stiffness about the way her body moves under the nightgown, as if she's holding herself straight.

"Well, tomorrow I'm gonna hit the road," I said.

Her eyes were still sleepy and the way she looked at me made me think that I was talking about a dream I'd had the night before.

"Whattaya mean?"

"Hitch-hiking, ya know. Thumbing." And I made the sign with my thumb.

"Oh," she said and started to break up a piece of toast until it was almost crumbs.

"You're not going to take the car?" she said.

"No I'm leaving that. Just my thumb."

"So Mommy and me can go on picnics," she said. She ate a piece of bacon slowly and looked away at some point down the hall-way.

"You could come with me if you wanted," I said. I'm going to live in the tent and take pictures everywhere I go. We could get a camera for you too."

She looked at me with that serious, examining expression, like old Benson at the firm gets when he has a shortage.

"I don't want to go," she said.

"But it'd be fun. We could fish, I'd get you your own fishing pole and at night you wouldn't have to get scared, sleeping right inside the same sleeping bag with me."

"I wouldn't get scared," she said.

And I knew she wouldn't. Only me.

"It'd be nice if you came," I said.

And then she said the craziest thing.

"Mommy'd be lonely if we both went."

"Sure," I said, because she was right, but I didn't know how to say it just wasn't fair.

It's hard to be honest with people. I mean I hadn't planned to take her in the first place. If I had I would have taken her with me when I bought my camera. I meant to go alone from the start and her refusal was just a formality. I suppose the thing that bothered me was that she had the words that made her sound more honest than me. That was the thing that wasn't fair.

So I arrived in Vancouver after three weeks of travelling alone. And I drank my whisky to celebrate that I did it. I'd got there on my own just like I did when I was 22 and I never phoned home once or even sent a post-card.

I walked back down the hill toward the beach. I saw and recognized monkey trees and dogwoods but I didn't know the flowers as well. There were so many plants and trees. Everything seemed so alive and it was hard to have a hangover. I saw a brown thing, wet and shiny-looking, stretched out at the side of the road, and I bent and touched it, and it shrank into a fat ball of something that looked like chewed licorice. A slug. I'd read about them but I'd never seen one before. But I recognized it and there were many more on the ground as I went down the hill.

I took down the tent and folded it up slowly. It was already dry. The sun was hot but still gentle. I put away everything in the knapsack except the sleeping bag, which I spread on the sand, and then I lay down to think.

I felt awful. A crazy kind of trembling in all of me but I liked it. It was a pain that was easily bearable but it blocked out everything else, like what was going to happen now? I was here and now the question why? I'd travelled a long way and put up with talking to a bunch of people who gave me rides just to get here, just so I could pitch my tent for one night on a beach and drink a pint of whisky and laugh to myself? And what was I going to do now? But the lovely trembling was there and all I had to say was tomorrow will be better. The pain was an explanation for everything.

There was a girl lying in the grass off to my right. There were other people around now besides her and the women gathering beer bottles, so I don't know why I kept staring in her direction except because of the colours. She had a yellow thing in her hands, it looked like a raincoat or a ground-sheet and she wore a bright red shirt with long sleeves and some kind of shiny blue pants. She sat rocking herself, with her hands joined under her feet, back bent, head bowed forward. She wasn't saying anything but she looked like she could be chanting.

I really do have trouble making friends, especially with new people. It's because I'm shy. Bernice gets so mad when I won't go to parties. People don't ask us much now anymore and I'm just as glad. I like to have a few drinks, watch the TV until I get sleepy and then read a book before I go to sleep. Bernice doesn't understand about books and she'd rather be with people. That's why Ruth is her friend and not mine. But there was something about that girl rocking off to my right that I had to know. I'd never had that kind of feeling before. I usually don't bother.

I got up and walked over to her. She didn't stop rocking but I knew she saw me. I stood for a few seconds but that was an awkward feeling and I knelt down so I could see her face. She was young. Younger than me but her face had lines and it looked tired, not the kind of tired from not sleeping, some other kind; Bernice sometimes looks like that and I know she won't talk much until that feeling goes away. The girl was younger than Bernice though.

"I'm really hungry," I said. I was. "You know any places close around here where I can get something?"

She stopped moving for a second and then scrambled to her feet so fast that when she answered me, I was sitting and looking up to where she was pointing.

"About a quarter of a mile down the beach, there's a stand. Hamburgers and stuff."

Her hair was tight against her head and gathered in the back with an elastic so a bit of it hung limply like an old dog's tail and it wasn't soft or even coloured like Bernice's. She didn't take care of it, I thought, but it reminded me of the sand a few feet away from us and I would have liked to touch it.

She stopped talking and pointing when I didn't say anything and she squinted her small eyes at me until they were just wrinkles in her face.

"You know, because your eyes are small it makes your mouth look ... bigger," I said. "Not bigger, I don't mean wide. I mean I notice it more because your eyes are smaller. You know what I mean?"

"No, do I have to?"

"No, I guess it doesn't matter except I kept wondering why I noticed your mouth so much."

"So it just matters to you."

"I guess so."

"And that's OK, isn't it?" she said and I felt stupid for having said anything and wondering why I did.

"I'm really starving," I said. "Are you hungry?"

"Starved."

"Can I buy you a hamburger?"

"And a coffee," she said, "I would love a coffee."

"OK," I said and began following her out on the beach. She walked not in the direction of the snack-bar but toward the sea and soon we were walking in the wet sand the sea had left. Her face was bent intently toward the ground.

"What're you looking for?" I said.

"Nothing in particular. I just like to look."

"I should bring back something for my daughter," I said.

"You've got a daughter?"

"Yeah, she's nine. Maybe she'd like a sea-shell."

"We can find plenty," she said and began bending and picking up things and handing them to me. While she looked all I could think of was Cathy and I tried to remember if she liked things like sea-shells. And I couldn't remember but I knew Bernice did.

"Are you visiting?" I asked to block everything out of my mind.

"Just passing through. You?"

"I'm going back to Toronto on the train tonight."

"Toronto?"

"Yeah."

"That's funny," she said. "I'm going to end up there sometime this summer. Depends on the rides."

"Where are you from?"

"Connecticut."

"In the States?"

"Yeah."

"You don't have an accent," I said.

"Neither do you." And I felt stupid again but glad I was with her and I looked at the yellow plastic sheet she sometimes carried or tied around her neck like a cape and I wondered where her other stuff was. She needed more things to travel. She couldn't walk very long wearing the rubber sandals on her feet. I wanted to know more about her but it didn't seem fair to ask when maybe there weren't any answers.

"Look at that beauty," she said and handed me a hard lump. The other shells I'd put in my pocket without hardly noticing them, except they were shiny with mother-of-pearl. This thing was dull and awful-looking with lumps all round, a shape that was vaguely like an oyster shell. But the oyster shells in my pocket I knew were beautiful, all ripply grooves and inside the jewel part that could be shined until it glowed.

"What's all that stuff?" I said.

"Barnacles. They've grown all around it so it's almost disappeared, but it's still there. It's really beautiful."

I put it in my pocket because I was fascinated that she liked it. I thought it was an ugly thing.

"It makes me think of all the stuff growing around here," I said.

"I don't understand."

"There's too much of it," was all I could say. "It kind of scares me. You know what I mean?"

"Maybe it's just because you're not used to being so close," she said, and I knew I should listen more clearly to what she said because I thought, because we're so different. Maybe, I thought, that's why I hate to meet new people, because I've got to listen. But the funny thing is that one of the things people are always saying to me, is what a good listener I am. Just because I don't talk much.

"Look at that guy and his dog," she said. "Aren't they lovely?"

I looked. That's a Dalmatian isn't it?" I said.

"I don't know but look at the way they walk together."

They were coming toward us. A young man, younger than me, with long blond hair, longer than the girl's, and him chasing the dog in circles so it was hard to say who was chasing who. The boy was so pale in the sun, like he was made of sand, his colour and smooth gliding movements, like sand running through your fingers and piling up at your feet. And the dog was dark and graceful and the two of them swooping in and out of each other's pattern of running were like waves to me.

"Good morning," the girl said as they rushed past us. And the boy turned and waved like a dancer.

"A great morning," he said.

"That's how I feel," I said.

And she stopped and looked at me with her squinty eyes and said firmly as if she was correcting me: "No, that's how he feels."

How can I explain it? She was a stranger and she said things like that to me. She was a strange girl but she made me smile there on the beach and there was a part of me that could have cried too.

We had french fries, two hamburgs each and I had a coke and she a coffee. She finished before me and waited. Then she stood up and while I was still sitting she stuck out her hand for me to shake.

"I gotta go," she said. "It's already late."

"Thank you," was what I said and then I laughed out loud and she did too. It was a huge sound that surrounded me and made me think of everything growing so close to us, the trees and plants reaching out, almost touching us, so alive and close.

"You're OK," she said.

And then she walked away and I couldn't see the back of her head because she used the yellow plastic to form a kind of hood and I watched the sandals flap against the soles of her feet for a long time until she was gone and after that I continued to hear the sound they'd made. Probably it was just the waves.

So now I'm on the train. Nothing is settled except that it will take me three days on the train to get back to Toronto and before I left I bought three bottles of whisky to help and I threw away all the shiny shells from my pocket. I kept the one with the barnacles and when I get home, I'll give it to Bernice. I hope she understands better than me.

THE HARBINGER

George McWhirter

On the seventeenth the smell of eggs is surmounted by that of the fowl. Not only chickens, however: it's Christmas, and geese, duck and turkeys dominate that corner of the market where he stands, watching you, appraising.

Now customers, countryfolk ... they will buy an egg unwashed or their poultry live because it sets a primitive seal on their freshness. And this was all he meant when he asked you how you'd like it. An unexpected option. But the seal is on your face: your grin must lead him on to say:

"Listen,"

and then to think: some interplay,

some pressure. Then with one hand he will hold you against him, and with the other undo the cord: the one that binds your feet more tightly than that which hobbles the turkey.

"Kill it yourself and you can keep it."

"And what if I can't?" you say while your eyes flicker, scatter before his breath as they did when he met you on the road. In summer, the gravel shuffling beneath your feet, your feet moving to a standstill, as now, as if caught in something thick and black

like tar.

"Then, I'll do you with this," he says, poking his pocket out.

"Only with that?"

Half buried in his shadow you don't care if you court

or tempt him so soon after you saw him with the other. So soon after you saw and heard the beak open and bubble between her legs, her throat rattle as if laden with beads: the prayer beads that fell, draining from her fist into the ditch.

Are you sure?

These coughs, which rake your chest like a hand searching in an empty barrel at the end of a voyage ... the spectre he sees in your blood, his reflection ... how real are they?

For years you have been disappearing, and then returning: a prodigal to yourself. Ever since that boy who joined the Brothers, the *Christian* Brothers. That adolescent, that redhead with acne, whose hands made hard and passionate love only in prayer. What could he press from that corruption: for which your father disowned you, for which you now disown yourself. And so you call yourself a tart. A tubercular tart, you laugh. And now you opt
for him
instead of clinic
or nuns.
Clearly.

The bird is male: scrawny and old. The only one he has brought, will ever bring. He looks across at the selection. There are hundreds. He watches their long necks rear up between the vans where they have been settled on straw, ready to be examined for plumpness, age ...

sex.

Particular attention is always paid to the breast. The width and depth. He reaches out, but fingers the brooch on your coat instead. The thing ... cheap like the coat, which is made from fake, black astrakhan. They both need cleaning.

"Here," he says.

The bird begins to jerk.

Slowly, you watch him circle. Like a scrutineer: up and down, whichever way for vantage point. Some farmers watch and their interest gratifies. It must make him feel like a promoter. See, how he points out the intricate lock you make with your thumb, middle and forefinger,

ready to jerk the neck from its housing. But as soon as the fingers tighten, the wings begin to thresh. You dig in heels. They skid, cobble
 by cobble,
 skid.
This novelty and the sight of your scrutineer amuses the folk: one will nod, another wink, someone shout an encouragement. Higher and higher rises your short plaid skirt. It's like a colourful circular wing. And sometimes, when the bird calms, like a parachute collapsing, or a tiny golfing umbrella: an umbrella your father gave you for the greens at Muckamore.

"How's that for sport?" some fellow shouts, some raw-boned youth who turns to watch the breadth of a farmer's hand bring you to a halt.

"Whoa there, Girl. You don't want to fly home so quick," he says.

"Get your hand out of it," you shout at him and cough.

"But my hand isn't in it," the farmer says. And whatever else you add causes him to swivel your body round.

"I think you came from over there," the farmer says.

Like a clockwork toy, redirected, but still out of control, your feet slither a few paces in his direction.

The sly merriment on the faces behind him acts as a brake. With a vicious twist you divide the slender, wrist-like conglomerate of bones, directing the gesture at the younger men and himself as if he has betrayed you. You hear your heartbeats, some change idling on a counter. Then, as if satisfied with this death, you dust your hands and gather up the bird in your arms. But as you pass, you begin to strut: you present him with your tongue. Red and round and mottled grey ... like an egg, which you juggle in its cup. And he laughs, laughs as you string the dead bird from a hook in an adjacent shed.

"Nice drumsticks," you hear someone remark.

"My drumsticks," he whispers, gripping the man at the top of his thigh, and the man feels something knotted deep like a cramp that attacks you for standing too long on that one leg.

But it's the back of your leg that's the draw. You remember reading how they were eaten in the camps, how you have good flesh: only your clothes, your lungs and mouth are bad. Especially the mouth: it has been used too loosely and too often. Like something else.

"A better view from here," he says, motioning them nearer the eggstall.

You set to.

But he's unsettling you. Quills, you know, when plucked straight will pock out cleanly, and you curse at each black nib that's left embedded.

"Come on, Maizie. What's your hurry?" you say to yourself (as if this were a name you used to refer to yourself on such occasions), and turning from your half-stooped position you can see the egg queue in agreement.

Like a flock distracted in the act of formation . . . the nape of the V at the counter: one of the arms, which is formed by those waiting to be served, half-turned toward you; and the other, those who have been, facing you completely as if flying backward into the whitewashed wall. A small group hovers around him in the centre.

"Want to see something special for your turkey?" you shout.

He laughs and evades a retort. Once a young boy in Fermoile . . . you asked him if he'd like to see something you'd never shown before. Aye, he said. My big turd in a jar, you replied. And then you remember your mouth, the nicotine stains on your teeth where he put his tongue.

You unpin a feather from the bird's breast.

A flip, the weight of a breath and its edge begins to razor back and forth, the perfect pattern for your kiss until it flutters in a draft of wind that stirs the turkeys in their yellow nests.

"Makes your old uncles crawl," some idiot remarks.

An arabesque is drawn with the next feather before you break and fit it across your teeth, introducing with this a clumsy flamenco.

Along the feather's edge you pass your tongue. Remembering the eyelashes: soft and sleek; the eyelid. . . .
Tighter
    and tighter your teeth clamp on the stem. Any
    one
    of your appointments—the calves,

cheeks—any
one will fit into the bowl
of his mouth. You think of him rolling you through his palms like a figurine, a soapstone figurine . . . like the one your brother sent from Canada.

But he doesn't budge.

You pick up the bird and balance it on your breasts. Next the legs. You angle these across a shoulder; you catch hold of the beaked head to act as chanter.

You play it like a bagpipe.

And now a herd of elders who stop and lean on their sticks or wipe their boots one against the other. Very softly you begin to chant *The Soldier's Song*, hoping for trouble from the Protestants when they hear the offensive strains of the Republic's national anthem. But their laughter is unanimous. Male.

"Honk, honk. Hewine, herine. Old ro-oosters are we . . . " the boys abuse the lyrics and join in behind as you circle him where he stands, collarless

dark hair,

dark face.

You circle, and every now and then someone makes a duckbill of their hand and snaps the rump of the person in front, making him leap. The one behind you blocks the others as he stops, pretending to pluck a feather from your rear, then after a swivel of his hips, he carries on the conga.

Then, passing in front of the shed a fourth time, you lift your leg to twirl it as close to his face as your leg permits, and at that moment the bird revives, breaks from under your armpit. Its short lateral flight sends you careening into a puddle.

There is a hush. Possibly they are allowing time to ascertain the damage and gauge the correct pitch for a guffaw that will cover this: the bird on its back, slamming the cobbles. You, your bottom three-quarters dunked in a puddle while the tail of your skirt and coat draw up water like blotting paper.

"Your lips must revitalize," he says. And his comment pricks the tiny skein of shock that alone holds back the laughter in their throats. You think he has taken control when he bends forward, offering his hand and saying: "You owe me."

You look up from the survey of your skirt.

"Yes."

With that you spread your legs, planting your feet well apart, making sure that they all can see the hair. As always it curls and beckons round the edges of your pants. Like bullocks, not quite grasping, but sensing what's at stake, the others circle close. And when you feel their nearness, you pull him forward until your mouth is level with his ear.

"Take me now if you want your turkey's worth."

"Go on," they say. "We'll hide you."

Of course they will hide and harbour him. They always have . . . .

Then, gripping your wrist, he turns on a youth who is squatted on the turkey and grinning like a gargoyle.

"Did you shit that or does it belong to me," he says.

He kicks out, strong enough to maim all of them, all at once, but he allows someone to grip his armpits: another hand to spiral up your skirt.

You can see the open doors of his van . . . dark paper he must have used to keep out light during the long turmoil of the journey . . . the paper still in place on the windows at the back. You remember his laughter as they lift you and set you down with your legs dangling out of the straw.

A glimpse

caught of him leaning to pick up the bird, then stopping to inspect the face he wears in a puddle. His hair, you remember, how it hangs like this man's in black veins from his brows, and the real one in his forehead that pounds like a subcutaneous extension.

His skin, like this, greasy to the touch; a few blackheads standing out on the cheek, very few, the weather burns them off, but it leaves a white ring like a collar on the flesh:

a roman collar.

The stud must dig into his Adam's apple as he looks up from the puddle, hearing something, remembering. The bird is dead, exhausted of interest, you think. Then, the doors swing open, and the man on top of your body hops out, leaving you belly-up in your yellow roost. Without changing position, but raising your head slightly, you spit at your lover and designate another.

"Here," he says. "You forgot something."

A clumsy larrup. The head skids on the roof, and coming down you see it for a moment, cocked absurdly to the side, as if trying to diagnose what goes on inside that dirty little dome.

Perhaps the touch of colour on your stomach adds a new attraction or

taboo, for though they crowd forward to look, no-one touches you, no-one makes a move to prevent him as he pushes round the side toward the driving compartment.

And he drives with a certain care.

Care. . . . Enough to worry, but not to damage, and by the time he stops his Black Maria, you have already climbed out and are waiting for him: the bird by the legs so that its head dangles on the ground and the blood cakes with muck and grit.

"It's about your size," he says, pointing to the head.

Up you swing. . . . A final gesture of dismissal, and for an instant the beak catches on his cheek, near the eye.

But nothing registers.

It's as if his flesh has been anaesthetized by the blood that drips from the bird's beak, or the apex of a finger in the wind that reminds him of his duty. Your face on the other hand has been laid open. One finger strays to the ring around his neck. He answers by gripping yours.

"A priest?" you ask and you would recite a rosary of desires, but his brow is as broad as the horizon. No shadow of a curl or cloud. He holds you an inch above the ground on a shallow meniscus of light. Already you pluck away the fake astrakhan, the skirt. He lowers you beside the other. An attempt is made to match its composure, but then you lose control. You rock from breast-bone to crotch. Soft as suet. Yielding to the final scissor in the sky.

MAGICIANS

Beth Harvor

He was showing her his recent past, slide after slide of it. She held small views of western streets and Rocky Mountains and Pacific Ocean up to the kitchen window's light. These were from his last trip. Now he was off once more, and would soon be bringing back the *east coast* for her to squint at—harbour by harbour and street by street. But now he was getting to the end of the box. He had saved the best one for the last.

"Here's quite a good one," he said, handing it to her between forefinger and thumb.

She thought it was good too. An old grey house down by a waterfront. On one side of the door the pale, peeling torso of a ship's figurehead—all blues, sick whites, the nose missing, the hair like badly-piled snakes. The remains of the face were placid; it was a face that gave distance its due. Also, the paint of the eyes had flaked off. And on the other side of the doorway, there was a tall narrow window, and behind the window, behind the smeared glass, a little girl with pale snaggy hair and a round deprived face. It seemed strange that a face could be so perfectly round and at the same time so perfectly deprived. Just as it seemed strange that she, Clare, should so often be unhappy in quite a different sort of house, in this house, here, where the sun shone on the handsome black-and-white tile floor (superimposing its own squares of light), where she could even look out into a garden while she washed the dishes—a beautiful garden (even as gardens go) and in winter beautiful too, in fact in winter a graphic garden, the black branches, the vertical black boards of the fences, all with their epaulets of snow. She looked at the little girl in her leaning sad beautiful blue-grey and probably smelly harbour house, and felt some guilt that she could find such a picture beautiful. Tourists were said to cope with the same kinds of feelings in places like Naples and in the poorer parts of Rome.

"It really captures the poverty and the fog," she said.

"It does," he said.

"Will you have your tea now then?" she asked him.

He shoved over his cup.

The tea sprang from the spout in a high clear arch.

"Like a little boy seeing how far he can make it go," she said.

"It is," he said. He looked at it down in the cup. "It *looks* like something done by a little boy, too," he said. "You never make it strong enough." He shoved it back to her. "For God's sake, Clare, steep it a little."

She steeped it till it looked like consommé.

"Is it OK now?"

"Better than it *was*, anyway."

From one extreme to the other, was what he was thinking though. He wished she wouldn't wear those over-sized sad sad cardigans. She had no right to look so vulnerable, so sloppy. Her face was very young looking, her straight hair was pulled back into an elastic band. But her stomach looked three months pregnant. She hadn't had a baby for years, all their children were now in school, and here she slopped around, forever looking three months pregnant. He found he was looking forward to the next lap of the tour and all the airline stewardesses.

"I hardly think about you when you're gone," she said. "I mean I never worry or wonder about what you're doing in the evenings, or anything."

"I never worry or wonder about what you're doing in the evenings, *either*," he said, "because I know you're never doing anything."

"I have a rich fantasy life," she said.

"I daresay you need it."

"When will you be back then?" she asked him.

"Two weeks."

Now he was gathered together at the door, and stood flanked by matching graduated luggage. His raincoat, on his arm, was folded neat as a flag.

"I love you," he said dutifully.

She couldn't bring herself to say anything one way or the other. So she tenderly patted his face.

He pried his tongue into her mouth when they kissed good-bye. But while he was kissing her she could feel him looking at the clock over her shoulder.

"I love you, I love you, I love you," Clare thought, walking in her high boots along the wet leaf-littered streets. It wasn't her husband she was thinking of, but somebody else's. A man who crawled on his stomach through her blood, kneed his way up and down her system, was on her, in her, night and day, in her mind. A speck of plane flew high overhead, very high up in that sky of stomach-dropping blue. Maybe it was the plane her husband was on, maybe he was at this very moment being lulled by aquamarine music, maybe he was at this very moment being leaned down to, being served airline cookies—little cellophane packs of scalloped circles stuck together with oversweet frosting fill and embossed with maple leaves. He could have them.

While she was making supper her children changed themselves into magicians. They came to the table with long black eyebrows and moustaches that went up into commas, and pointed black beards. They kept making faces at her. "God, you look repulsive," she told them. They were delighted. They couldn't hear it often enough.

"Are we really repulsive?" they kept saying.

"Yes," she kept saying back.

And at bedtime, as she was wiping the black from the face of one of them, from the face of Martin, the oldest one, she was thinking of the husband of her friend. Her desire for him was quite unbearable sometimes. She was thinking of how she loved him, when suddenly, without warning, she said out loud, "I love you." Her son, thinking it was meant for him, smiled at her so sweetly.

Swept by guilt, she held him to her for a moment, terribly tightly.

Her friend's husband was named Don. An ordinary name. An ordinary person. No! Not an ordinary person! Not even ordinary-*looking* once you got to know him. And *he* had such a way of looking at people. Or at least he had such a way of looking at her. A look that took you in entirely, enclosed you. She remembered being a small child and standing barefoot on a sheet of brown paper while her father held a pencil up close against each foot, and described each foot with the pencil, so that he could take the pictures of her feet out in his pocket and come back bringing new shoes. She had been delighted with those pictures of her feet. The way Don looked at her, she felt he saw her exactly as she was, his look described her, and yet she felt such deep approval in his eyes. He treated her with the gentle courtesy one might show to a beloved child. She remembered she had gone to their house to deliver something, some books, late one raining Sunday afternoon. And she had stood out on their white porch with the sky all dark behind her, and her maroon leather shoes had been rained on till they had turned the colour of wine, and she had been shaking the rain out of her coat when he had opened the door to her, but she hadn't been able to shake the happiness out of her eyes. She had always felt that he was ten times more interesting and ten times less pretentious than anyone else. And apart from that, and apart from all the sexual feeling, she had always felt that he was *good*. He had held the door open for her and she had preceded him into the summer dimness of his house. And there had been such a curious smell in the interior of that house, a smell of old socks and fallen flowers. His wife was away. She had known that, known that, known that, when she had cunningly come, returning his books. She didn't see any of the old socks, but she saw little collars of fallen petals around all the vases in the living-room. In the kitchen there was a little more light. Not much, but a little. Big windows looked out into a garden of soppy tropical greens and the rain dribbled down them while he put on water for tea.

"Which tea will it be?" he had asked her. "Formosa Oolong? Lapsang Souchong? Jasmine? St. John's Wort?"

They had decided on a blend of Jasmine and St. John's Wort.

"St. John's Wort is like a field of hay," he had said. "You're not allergic to hay, are you?"

No, she had assured him, she wasn't allergic to anything. And she had hoped this would raise her stock with him. The Jasmine flowers had floated like bits of discoloured paper among the grasses in her cup of tea.

And some time later, walking home in the rain, past all the sopping wet gardens, she had felt that she should think some sobering thoughts and douse the happiness in her face before she got back to her husband and children.

On the porch she had taken off her shoes, squeaky with wet, and had come into the house barefoot. A wet-footed, white-footed, barefooted truant. But her children had been watching television and her husband had been reading the paper. They had hardly looked at her at all, and she had gone into the kitchen to start supper, pirouetting as she had cooked and cleaned up, leaping across the chess-board linoleum floor with a violent silent joy. And the happiness inside her! But now she was safer with it. She could push it out of her face and back onto a secret simmer and make it last for hours and no-one would know it was there. She felt happy the way a child can feel happy—without a reason, without knowing a reason and with no need to know a reason.

And so she had sometimes seen him since. Him and his wife, Frances, who was her friend. Frances appreciated him, anyone could see that. And besides, Frances was a warm and attractive person herself. And so Clare went on, would go on forever, feeling that way about him, feeling that deep submerged bond between them, but nothing would ever come of it.

Now all the magicians were asleep. Their moustaches and beards had been creamed away, their faces were upturned, fair, flushed, flung this way and that. She was getting ready for bed herself, had brushed her hair, had figure-eighted an elastic band around it, and was now standing in front of the bathroom mirror, clowning her face with cream. The nightly circus of the no-longer-young. Next week she was invited to a party where Don and Frances would also be. She would wear her African print dress, and her hair hanging straight, and she would be feeling too happy to need jewelry. She was *that* young, anyway, that she could still get by on clean hair and happiness. Downstairs, the phone rang, making her jump. She ran down into the coldness of the hall. She jerked one of her husband's old raincoats off a hanger and was still working herself into it as she picked up the receiver and said hello.

"May I speak to Clare Stanzel?" A man's voice asked her.

"Clare Stanzel speaking."

"Clare! Is it really you?"

"Yes," she said, "but who's this?"

"Someone who loves you very much."

That narrows the field, she thought, but it was not a voice she recognized.

She said: "There can't be that many people who love me very much."

He said: "There can't be that many people who love you as much as *I* do."

A pause followed this gallant remark.

"Keep saying nice things," she instructed him finally, "maybe after a while I'll figure out who you are."

He laughed and then she knew him.

"Wilf Dasgupta!"

"Wilf Dasgupta it is," he said, sounding even more delighted than she did.

"Good to hear from you, Wilf."

"It's been too long," he said. "How's Rawge?"

"Rawge is well. Travelling at the moment."

"And the children?"

"Sleeping. But they're fine too. They were magicians at supper tonight."

"Magicians," he said. "And you?"

"Pardon?"

"And how are you?"

"All right," she said. "Fine. Very well, as a matter of fact."

A skeptical silence ensued. She remembered how he used silences to browbeat you into confessing how you *really* felt. She felt a need to quickly pour words into the void.

"It's strange, I was thinking of you just the other night," she said. She knew he would like that. And besides, it was true.

"What were you thinking?"

"Well, you remember that beautiful art book you gave us when we were married?" she asked him. "We still have it," she continued—she was making it sound as if they made a practice of throwing their beautiful art books out with the garbage or something—"and I was just passing by the bookshelf—"; by now she was wishing she had never started on this, for her thought of Wilf as she had passed by the bookshelf had been a feeling of irritation at the tyranny of his love, at his insistence on beauty, and she had even taken the book down and had read the impassioned dedication he had written to her and Roger on their marriage, telling them how beautiful they were, how miraculous it was that these two beautiful people should have found each other and should now be joined together, and she had closed the book with a real slap of anger. "And?" Wilf was saying, pleased as punch, by now certain he sniffed the scent of a beautiful dénouement. "Well, I noticed how it—how the book—was sticking a little out from the shelf—" She paused, by now regretting her whole contribution to this conversation. She wanted quickly to finish it. She finished: "—and so I shoved it back in."

"That's what you do to me," Wilf said in a heavy swinging voice, "shove me back on the shelf."

She couldn't answer this. She could only think of Wilf in his Montreal studio. Of his tender drawings of nude pregnant negresses up high on the walls. Of the dark nipples, sturdy as gumdrops, hung in the gleaming brown slings of the breasts. Of Wilf, standing barefoot, serving, at just the right moment of the day, when the sun lay across the low black table in the strong-smelling studio, the little glasses of apricot brandy that went down the throat with an oversweet slippery sting. Of the holes at the shoulder of his shirt where his pet bird sometimes sat and clawed. Of the free-form bird-cage he had made for the bird, but which the bird had never taken to. Of an older black wire bird-cage (which the bird had never taken to either), that Wilf had later converted into a portable liquor cabinet, housing half a dozen tall-necked bottles, and of how he used to swing the cage back and forth in front of them, saying, "What'll you have? Port? Sherry? Madeira?" And then he would sing in a cracked satanic Bengalee falsetto, "Have some Madeira, my dear ...," and she remembered too his great bowls of fruit that he washed at the old sink where he apparently also washed himself and mixed his paints, and of how good the fruits always looked when he brought them round, clear-beaded with water. And later, coming down into the suppertime dark and the snow-thickened streets, they had felt their eyes were over-tired, over-bright, that everything about Wilf and his studio always came on too strong—the dogmatic batiks, the tangled plants, the raucous tyrannical bird. Even the tenderness of the nude pregnant negresses, up there on the walls in small worlds of their own, even that came on too strong. And Wilf had played ragas long before anyone else, long before they had become fashionable in the West, for his father had come from Bombay, and the fact that his mother was a hard-shell Canadian baptist hadn't cancelled this out. In fact, in Wilf, nothing had been cancelled out.

"Clare," Wilf was saying, with a kind of deliberate urgency on the other end of the telephone line.

She hugged the raincoat very tightly around her and waited.

"Clare, you know I care for you and Rawge very much."

"Yes, Wilf."

"But about *you*, Clare, *for you*, Clare, I've always felt something very special, ever since I first met you, ever since you opened the door to me that time when you were staying at the Weinbergs'. . . . How old were you then, Clare? Twenty? You were very beautiful then, you know that, and you also know, and *I* know that *you* know, that I don't mean beauty in any outside ordinary surface sense, I mean *real* beauty." He paused a moment. His voice had begun to sound charged. He said finally: "I felt that you were good."

"But I'm a mixture of good and bad!" she cried. "Like everyone else!"

"I know what I know," he said, in his inscrutable stubborn voice. There was both Bombay and baptist in that voice.

"I think you tried to put some kind of halo around me," she said.

"No, no! I didn't try to sanctify you, I didn't try to deify you, I just know what I saw! I feel that there's a place in *my heart* for you, just as there is a place in *your heart* for me, that no-one else will ever occupy, in either of us; that there is an area, a territory, a *country*, if you like, where only you and I meet. A spiritual bond, if you like."

She didn't know if she liked or not. Still she felt a need to say, "Wilf, would you care to come over and have some tea or something?"

"Clare, I'm here for the opening of an exhibition of a friend of mine. You remember my good and beautiful friend, Jean-Luc? Yes? Well, he's having a one-man show here at the Wells Gallery, and now here I am at a party in his honour, here at the Boyds', until I take the train back very late tonight."

There was a pause.

"But to hell with the party!" he cried suddenly. "*You* are more important than a party! I'll come and see you!"

Clare didn't see how a cup of tea could compete with a party. Even a cup of tea with her. Aloud she said: "I don't want to take you away from your party, Wilf." This was the truth.

"But of course I'll come!" he insisted. "One moment. Someone here drives me over. Can you hold the line?"

She could hold the line. She could also suddenly hear a great avalanche of talk in the background, as if double doors had just been opened. Then, after a time, the talk stopped; the double doors must have closed. She heard him pick up the phone again.

"Clare," he said. Now his voice sounded low, confidential. He sounded like some sort of salesman. "There seem to be some complications here, my little one, so I don't think I'll be able to see you this time, but I'm going to be writing to you."

"Fine, Wilf. I look forward to seeing you another time. It's pretty late right now anyway." Again true.

"Why haven't you ever written to me?" he demanded suddenly. His voice was strong with claims.

"But Wilf, I never write to *anyone*."

"But that's putting me with everyone else!"

Dammit, he *was* with everyone else. This time she refused to answer.

"Clare," he said, after a silence, "Will you do something for me?"

"I'll try," she said warily. She wanted to know what it was first though.

"Remember that I love you," he said.

"Yes, Wilf, thank you, I'll remember."

"I love you."

"Yes, Wilf, thank you. And thank you for calling." By now she was feeling very old.

"Good-bye then, Clare."

"Good-bye, Wilf," she said, and she quickly put down the phone. And then she fled, actually fled, up the stairs, pulling the old raincoat off her as she ran, and pelting it into a pile of dirty laundry at the top of the stairs. Then she bounced onto her bed, and pulled the covers up quickly before she had time to get cold. She snapped out the light, and lay at attention under the blankets.

But inside her, her heart was beating like a mad bird in the cage of her ribs. And for a long time she couldn't get to sleep. She knew Wilf's need to think he loved people. She knew how he needed to think that things were beautiful and good. She knew it didn't have anything to do with her, any more than the fact that his paintings shone out at you had anything to do with the canvas they were painted on. But this is what bothered her, lying there in the bed: if it didn't have anything to do with her, and if it didn't mean anything, then why did she feel so angry? And why did she feel as if something had been taken away from her? Why were her eyes stinging in her cold-creamed face? Why did she feel as if she had been robbed?

ONE FOR THE ROAD

John Sandman

Nick told the salesman from Toronto to go to hell and slammed the door of his 68 Mustang and walked back to the intersection. After he'd gone a few car-lengths it occurred to him that he hoped the window broke after he slammed the door but when he looked over his shoulder to see, the car had disappeared in a cloud of shimmering heat and he was there alone again in Thunder Bay. He didn't feel any less alone sitting across from that gearbox salesman with his Mustang talking about money all the way through from Sudbury, Nick talking about being out of work, the salesman talking about all the stuff he could buy on credit, Nick talking about being broke, he knew if they kept that up he'd get into a fight sooner or later. When they made Nipigon the salesman said well after all this talk about you having no money and me having it all why don't I stake you to a few hamburgs, I'm starving. Nick said that's swell by me, how you spend your money is your business, realizing afterwards how that sounded when this guy had just burned up the last six seven hundred miles talking about money. The guy came back with a double dunked in cheese Lakehead burger and a black-and-white shake saying it's all yours fella. Nick looked at this shit like it fell out of the sky but not for long and put it away like it was his last meal. He was in the middle of telling the guy how the last meal he had was back on the job in Toronto about fifteen minutes before they came and laid him off when this gearbox salesman starts spouting all this shit about how he doesn't feel like hearing about all that bloody hard luck and trouble nonsense and if he was nice enough to buy Nick something to eat the least he could do was talk about what he wanted to talk about. Nick almost choked on his black-and-white shake and said you can shove the rest of this shit up your ass if you think I'm going to sit still and listen to that business. Now Nick was back on the highway leaning up against the prop wash from the endless line of semis and moving vans that turned up highway seventeen from Thunder Bay and the States. He couldn't get over the way this guy with the Mustang and those fancy gearbox clothes acted like he was a big deal buying Nick a hamburg after he got done with saying how loaded he was. He didn't say a word the rest of the way after Nick told him to get stuffed. If the guy's got money, it's no surprise if he buys somebody a hamburg, why should he act like you owe him something if he's so good at throwing it around.

Nick looked around the highway. There were about five guys in back of him about a mile down and nobody in front of him, first in line, at least something good came of that last ride, thinking he shouldn't have to wait too long when up ahead a station wagon pulled over and let off four fuckin' guys with army-navy stores strapped on their backs. Nick picked up a two-by-four in case they got any ideas about jumping ahead in line though with four guys he'd watch his step if he had to. He watched them clank by pots and pans tied to their belts like Fuller-Brush men from Mars with big green jackets and boots and hair that looked like it was made from Brillo pads. They never looked up from the road, they didn't even act like they knew where they were, Nick thinking holy shit I hope I get where I'm going to that job in Vancouver before I get like that. He lost track of them as they kept walking on and not seeming to get any further away. Put down the two-by-four. More semis, tankers pushing all the way to Winnipeg in ninth, every once in a while Nick could hear one drop it back in second as it got off the red light and almost die up the hill from the intersection, whisking along beer cans and shake cartons by the side of the road. A column of rigs shimmering across the intersection jerked from their regular speed when a duffle bag went flying across the front bumper of a semi and a guy with it picking it up off the ground as it hit the road, kicking it all the way up to the intersection before he put it on his back. Nick picked up his two-by-four. He had earrings, long dungarees with suspenders, no shirt no shoes and his hair stuck out three inches on the sides. Nick really took this guy for some kind of gearbox who didn't know how to cross the street, away from home for the first time let alone hitch a ride, saying how's hitch-hiking as he walked by, Nick grunting and right then a VW stopping in front of Nick, gathering up his gear running straight for it and just when his ass hit the cushion the back of the seat pushed forward that same gearbox with earrings and suspenders landed right in back, the driver looking confused then saying oh well might as well get both, putting it in gear and pulling away. The kid in suspenders started talking a mile a minute about shitman I can really dig VW's I just came up from the States where they got a zillion of 'em—some American suck eh thought Nick wanting to pound the shit out of him but it wasn't his car and he hung back instead, listening to him saying to the driver got any spare change it would be the most beautiful thing in the world if you could lay a nickel on me or a quarter or five dollars, pointing to a window envelope on the sun visor—hey ya got your paycheck that means you can lay some pretty heavy bread on me huh —the driver turned and looked at both of them and said I don't know who you guys are but I'm not listening to that spare-change drivel from here to Winnipeg, this is as far as you guys go, Nick blurting out that he didn't know who this gearbox was but he wouldn't say a word for a thousand miles—Nope, I said out and I mean out. The driver opened the door, the kid with suspenders jumping out first. Nick wanted to really pound him now, but he kept walking down the road instead of jumping ahead of him like Nick thought, Nick moving down a little ways himself. As soon as the kid put his pack down he unhooked the suspenders and started pacing up and down the road talking to himself. There was a general store across the road with hoses ripped off the gas pumps all boarded up with a closed sign. He ran across the highway up the steps pounding on the door yelling back at Nick, did he think it was open, did he think they sold tobacco, running back to the road pacing up and down like an expectant father pointing at deserted garages yelling at Nick did he think they were closed. When some local boys came cruising down the highway they slowed up at where the kid stood then laid some rubber for a hundred yards. They turned around and cruised past him three or four more times and stopped the fifth time. Nick saw one of them get out and said that's the end, never see that freak alive again, starting the three-mile walk down the highway back the other way to the intersection trying not to hear if they were pounding him up like he knew they were. There was a big valley in the road for a while and it made for quite a hike, Nick stopping for a pop on the way spending some of his last change. Toward the intersection he saw the same people he did when he first got there. They were going to Banff in Alberta looking for work, another guy walking past saying the best place for work was Northern Alberta where they're laying a lot of petroleum pipes. This guy kept going down the road when a semi-cab stopped for him before he got 50 yards away and the two going to Banff swore up and down why didn't that happen to them, Nick walking back to the intersection to get his old place in line. There was still nobody within a mile of it.

There weren't as many tourist family types going by as there were in the Soo. Some drove by waving at him but he couldn't figure out what for and they kept on going. A truck coming up from the South that Nick didn't see until the last minute hung a left and stopped right at Nick's feet. It was one of those camper jobs with Massachusetts on the plates—where the hell was that? Down East? Nick didn't give a shit, it looked like it would be some family that might set him up to some meals. The rig had a big door almost like it was a converted step-van. The door slid back and there was this guy with hair all down his back and a beard. Nick was glad to see him in a way except he expected a different kind of person to be there, it made Nick mad to see that it looked like he was thinking the same thing, standing by the doorway not knowing if he should sit down.

"Go on ahead sit down, where are you going?"

"Er, I'm going out to Vancouver."

"Oh really? Well you're in luck, we're going to California."

"All the way out there eh?"

"By the way, my name's Richie, this is Ted in the back there."

"I'm Nick."

"Is your name Nick or Nicholas?"

"Well it's uh Nick. Nick Leslie."

"Oh, what brings you all the way out here?"

"I uh, I'm looking for a job."

"What for? A summer job?"

"No I'm looking for work."

"Oh making ends meet huh. Working your way through school? Are you an engineering student?"

"No, just looking for a job."

"What for, I don't understand?"

"I'm gonna have to make some money to live on."

"I don't understand, what do you mean live on, what are you living on now?"

"I have a few dollars left from my last pay."

"Really? Far out. What do you do?"

"I'm looking for work, I—"

"—Oh that's a bummer."

"Yeah I try to manage—"

"Are you Canadian?"

"I'm from Toronto."

"What's it like living up here compared to living in the States? Pretty groovy huh? It's legal to smoke dope up here isn't it?"

"I don't know about that, I haven't heard anything—"

"What do you mean, I don't understand."

"I mean, yah see, I've been working in er, a factory for the past three or four years—"

"What do you mean, I don't understand, why work in a factory?"

"I gotta make a living—"

"—Do you have any careers in mind?"

"Like what?"

"I don't know, I'm asking you, there must be managerial positions in the firms you work for. You might even meet some groovy people who'd pick you up that could put you in touch with a career."

"Yeah? You know anyone like that? Is that why you're on the road?"

"Uh no I don't think so, ha ha. If I were the sort of uh person who could supply you with that sort of service I wouldn't be here. You mean a career counsellor. Uh no this is my vacation."

"Hey Richie do you think we have room for one more?"

"Uh just a minute—uh Nick I'll get back to you in a minute, don't worry we'll get our heads together about this—What Ted?"

"Think we have room for one more?"

"Sure."

Nick sat back to relax until he'd have to start listening to Richie again worried because he never knew how to act around these people, when he realized who they might be picking up. He sat up like a sprung rat-trap and was going to tell them don't whatever you do pick up the creep with suspenders but the truck stopped, Nick figuring he couldn't say anything since it was their truck a couple American college dinks then in came the pack and then the kid, suspenders and earrings and all the other shit, bare feet, the driver saying farout, how's it going on the road, the kid saying bad scene bad scene I've been lucky so far since I got my hair cut, some stud I knew in Colorado two cowboys stopped him when they saw his hair and beat the shit out of him, I don't understand these long-haired dudes going out on the road they give me a set of bad vibes—the other two guys looking at each other fiddling with their braided hair thinking maybe we oughta see where this guy's head is at before we decide how far we want to ride with him. They both had long hair but you could tell this kid just cut his off by the way it hung above his ears, it looked like a girl's hair who just had a pixie cut, parted in the middle. The two long-hairs didn't know how to take this kid, looking over some mileage chart, but the kid snapped his suspenders acting like he owned the place asking where are you from, the two long hairs saying Massachusetts, the kid saying I bet you came up here because you thought it would be a fuckin groove—That's mainly why we came up here, yeah—Well you really got ripped off man, there's nothing but bare land up here, hills, lakes, valleys, streams, I ain't seen anything that looked close like a city since I left Toronto except there was some pretty farout factories in Sault Ste. Marie and pile drivers and scrap iron and shit but since then there's been nothin if you don't count the grain elevators in Thunder Bay, this ain't a country, this is the sticks, I ain't seen a subway since I left Philadelphia, letting a few billboards go by then saying oh that's right my name is Cal and I'm from Delaware. Nick stuck out his hand from force of habit, the others not sure what he was trying to do, then they shook hands all around, Cal giving Nick a fish like he hoped and Nick clamped a real handshake on him, Cal screaming like somebody hit him with a hammer what are you some paranoid fucker trying to act heavy with me, you don't like the kind of trip I'm on well don't act so heavy with me—glancing at the others for help—when people get uptight they do uncool things like put people through changes if you're trying to rip me off I'm not gonna help you by putting out bad vibes—Cal took out four sticks of dope cigarettes, the driver saying farout something to smoke—They each started drawing it in and blowing it out, Nick trying to be one of the boys and in five minutes the windows got all steamed up, Nick starting to feel real sick inside like he had some kind of cheap booze can wine and began to shiver all over, the others staring at him like he was a worse freak than them. Nick started to pile through his laundry bag to get something to hide his face in so these dinks wouldn't stare at him and he wouldn't be cold. He almost fell through the open door of the truck when he pulled out his blue and white high-school jacket with SHEET METAL lettered on the back—he was shivering less after it was draped around his head. Cal lifted it up off his head and dropped it back—There see what I mean he's uptight, I told you it was uptight up here, you're like that cop he's like that cop hassling me at customs, I was tryin' to hitch-hike across the border with my dogs and because of that they wouldn't let me in the country, see how paranoid that is, they don't even dig animals—Nick saying from underneath his jacket that's all BS, we like animals in Canada, sure we like animals up here, I like animals, I had animals, a dog once—Cal saying you're shinning me on or how come the customs man wouldn't let me in the country if Canadians like animals, he called my dog a filthy pig and that was a rip-off—I bet it had rabies, Nick trying to button the jacket around his head—that does it you're just uptight when it comes to animals, you can't dig animals so don't try to tell me different, you're so paranoid you got your jacket over your head you don't want people to see you when you're stoned—Nick shaking mad underneath the jacket wanting to rip it off and shove it down his throat—You know if you don't like it why don't you go back where you came from, the long hairs saying you guys are getting pretty violent considering all this dope you've smoked—Tell this gearbox to go back where he came from—Take it easy Nick nobody's going to bother you, why don't you relax and take your jacket off your head, Nick taking it off and putting it over his shoulders grabbing onto the door jamb as the truck swung around a corner, long shadows falling across the road from the forests, a half-dozen hitch-hikers going by the road every quarter-mile. Cal started muttering something about animals, paranoid people are so much more uptight than animals and Nick started laughing like somebody was tickling him, Cal saying still uptight about your problems huh Nick even when I tickle you you stay uptight, what are you laughing at now that's making you all paranoid —Ted in the back saying he's laughing because you're tickling him—Cal screaming so what, does that mean he has to laugh just because somebody tickles him, everybody laughing his ass off, Cal screaming you fuckers give off a set of bad vibes I ain't talking to nobody or tickling nobody no more boy if I had my dogs here it'd be different.

They drove all night through Ontario, Nick noticing how much it looked exactly like all the other shit he'd seen so far. When was this gonna end? Where the hell was Vancouver? They gave Nick a turn at the wheel and he pushed it as fast as he could get away with up over the hills and through blind curves until the other guys were yelling at him to cool it. As long as he was moving on the highway he promised himself to get there as fast as possible as long as he knew there was a job at the other end of the road. Handing the wheel over to Richie he remembered that these guys said they were going to California. Did that mean they were going down through the States pretty soon or straight out to Van? If they weren't going straight he thought he better get off the first chance he got and dump these gearboxes, looking out the window as the darkness came closer to the truck hoping they were going straight so he wouldn't have to move from the truck till he hit Van, just like walking around the block from here on.

The dope started to wear off and the sun began to come up. Nobody said a word all night except to change drivers. Richie said he was getting hungry and it reminded Nick of the last time he ate back on the job in Toronto right before he got laid off, or right after. Two days ago. They pulled off by a lake just as the sun was coming up, Richie saying the thought of another day would never let them sleep and they'd have to drive another twelve hours before they could get any rest. Out of the truck Richie and Ted started pulling stoves and camping equipment out the back while Nick stood around trying to figure out what to do, watching Cal piss in the lake, Richie asking if hotdogs and baked beans was OK for breakfast. It was OK with Nick, offering to help with the cooking and peeling onions, the food waking them up. They had everything in the truck, knives, forks, plates, glasses, a refrigerator, Richie saying there was something pretty weird about Cal. Nick saw his chance to get on the good side of these dinks—Yah he sure is a real suck, I don't know why we don't get rid of him. Yeah said Richie, he talks like he was some kind of speed freak. I don't know, I was on speed studying for my finals and I didn't talk to anybody for days. Still he's pretty weird. Yah, Nick pouring the coffee, he don't know fuck all about much eh? Right when he slung the beans and franks on the plate Cal came back took one look at the food and said he didn't eat sugars or starches. Nick said all right this is beans and franks, it's good for yah, Richie and Ted looking at each other and saying oh, you're on a macrobiotic trip, that's outasight Cal, how long have you been doing it? Ever since I got my head together I don't eat any wasted products—Wasted products?—By wasted products I'm referring to that kind of shit the body don't use. Oh I see. I suppose that's a pretty healthy diet, Nick sitting back and watching the two long-hairs make Cal a whole new meal without sugars or starches, Cal saying the body don't need vitamin C either and dumped his grape juice on the ground. That was all Nick could take, jumping up and saying who the hell are you to throw away food when somebody offers it to you. Cal glanced at Nick—Bum trippin again huh man? If you don't like the food you can always go buy your own, you look like you can afford it. Nick was speechless, everyone else stopped what they were doing and took a long look at Nick. He looks like he could do a straight job huh man said Cal, Nick not moving a muscle waiting for Cal to touch his grape juice so he could dump him on the ground.

Ted stayed in the driver's seat most of the morning all the way to the Manitoba border by ten o'clock, everybody taking catnaps. Nick watched Cal for a while and was convinced he was out of his fucking tree, and was sure he could turn the two long-hairs against him and they'd all throw him out when they got to Winnipeg. An hour from Winnipeg they pulled over to get some cheap groceries and Nick noticed that Cal wasn't chipping in but back in the truck he sure was getting to the food like there was no tomorrow. Nick started to say how about saving some for us—That's OK Cal do your thing man said one of the long-hairs. Nick was gonna say wait a minute but thought about that ride straight across they could give him and shut up. When they saw how much food Mr. Cal Freako from Delaware was eating they'd lay the law down to him and he'd be on their good side at last. The land started to flatten out for Winnipeg, Nick feeling on top of it now that they were almost there and after Winnipeg Vancouver. Suburbs scattered by with railroad tracks slipping in between then weedy houses like you'd see at the end of a city around a few corners and dozens of huge concrete buildings popped out of nowhere at Portage and Main. It was slow going through city traffic, Cal getting bored eating up more food out to the end of the city, it looked like they were going back the way they came with nothing but flat land all round. Nothing on the highway. Richie said the plan was to get to Saskatchewan before night if they pushed it, Nick asking where the hell was Vancouver. Vancouver? We aren't even into the prairies yet, we got another couple thousand miles to go. Nick got exhausted looking at the map, the end of the page just touching the beginning of the prairies. Cal started talking his head off, asking if they were gonna drive all night and all day and all night again so they could get to a free rock and roll festival in Calgary, asking for food, asking for cigarettes, asking Nick for spare change, he never shut up, asking how to spell Saskatchewan, the two long-hairs saying far out outasight every time he opened his mouth. Nick noticed also that he never drove, they said because he was too young. He was old enough to ask for spare change. Nick panicked at the thought that Cal was getting on the good side of the freaks, thinking maybe they'd get together and throw him out. When it was his turn at the wheel he never took his foot off the gas, racing a few freight trains and Ted telling him to take it easy, Nick pretending not to hear him (take what easy?) or loudmouthing about how he used to take a double-axle Mack diesel on the Toronto-Hamilton-Windsor run from the plant, trying to put the accelerator through the floorboard and they were flying into Regina by the time the half-swampy greenish prairie night fell over the land. The highway seemed like dirt right up to the Parliament Buildings, stopping in the city for some groceries, Cal hitting Nick for spare change as soon as they walked into the store, the two long-hairs giving him bad stares when he didn't come across with it. Nick was afraid to ask Cal why he didn't ask them figuring that would play him off against the rest, Ted taking Nick aside saying we know you have a little money, could you help us out with the gas? Nick didn't know what to say but yes, afraid if he didn't come across they'd throw him out, but if he shelled out now they might appreciate it and realize later that Cal was taking them for a ride and not the other way around, then the three of them could throw Cal's bum out. Thinking about it made Nick giggle as he passed a deuce on to Ted and they drove North to find a place to park for the night. Earth-movers lined the highway on either side with roadbeds for new lanes being built, driving up the dirt road to a Provincial Park Nick snagged a couple of kerosene lanterns at a detour and they set them up to cook with, hustling so they wouldn't have to eat in the dark. After supper they all went off to piss except Nick who sat by the lanterns waiting for the mosquitoes to drive him into the truck. Nick started to make vague plans about what he'd do when he got to Vancouver but got side-tracked into thinking about what he was going to do about Cal. It was too late to try and tell them he didn't have any money after he'd been shelling out all this time. It was making him mad that he got all the way out here for a job and now he had to waste his time trying to figure out how to handle these dinks. He tried to turn his attention back to when he got to Vancouver, but there wasn't much he could do till he got there except watch his money and that meant watching these guys, and thinking about getting rid of Cal pushed everything else out of his head. The only other thing he could think of was telling that salesman with the Mustang to fuck off in Thunder Bay and was that ever a mistake. He couldn't afford to fuck himself up this time, even though he half felt that if he could get Cal out of his sight maybe it would be worth fucking up the ride with the long-hairs. No he did that already with the salesman, he had to keep control of himself with these guys. After all these guys weren't looking down on him like he didn't have any money like the salesman, in fact they acted like he was rich, even if he wasn't, so he could use this as a reason not to get mad at them. He sat there steely-eyed peering around the smoky kerosene lanterns into the night, trying to see where they were, maybe they were hiding somewhere, stealing his clothes out of his laundry bag.

"Boo! Surprised ya huh?"

"Oh—it's uh Richie."

"Yeah. The mosquitoes certainly are getting thick aren't they?"

"Yah phew. Sure would like a brew to wash these uglyass-tastin bugs down with."

"Would you like some mosquito-repellant?"

"Anything you have."

"Just spray it anywhere. You know we can't find Cal."

"Is that right?"

"I can't imagine where he could have gotten to. He annoys me when he pulls stunts like that, spending a half an hour in the men's room when we stop for gas. He's a pain, it'll be outasight when he gets off."

"Where's he getting off?"

"I don't know. I hope he doesn't think we're taking him home with us."

"You sure don't discourage him from anything."

"I know, I think people should be nice."

"Why don't you ask him when he's getting off? I bet he tells you to fuck off, that's how nice he is."

"Why are you always putting him down?"

"I'm not doing anything, ask him and see what happens."

"You're right. If I could convince him not to be such a pain I wouldn't be hassled into thinking I want to get rid of him."

"He's better having you talk to him than gettin' picked up by some truck driver who'd knock his brains out if he acted weird."

"Look man I'm not interested in hearing about some uptight truck drivers. If somebody'd do a thing like that, they're the ones with problems, not Cal."

"What about us though, we're the ones who put up with him if he rides with us."

"I, I can't throw him out. I expect people to be groovy to each other. Cal doesn't have his head together regardless of what he'd tell you. He's a victim of technology and like we have to be especially groovy to these people. He has no money, but he tries to be creative."

"Yah, what about all that food he ate we just bought, he ate practically every—"

"—Yeah but you can at least work in a factory, what can he do except what he's doing now? I think he's trying very hard to succeed in what he's doing, and we have to make allowances for those less fortunate—Oh shh here they come—"

Cal and Ted turned up the road toward the truck. Nick couldn't think of anything to say. The only thing he could say was that he didn't have any money or any job in a factory, not yet anyway. Fuck them, why should he tell 'em. They'd probably rate him with that dink Cal, he hadn't fallen that far even if he had to ride on the same truck with him.

Next morning they flipped a coin. Ted won and he pushed it all the way to Moose Jaw in a half-hour, driving around it the way they should have with Winnipeg instead of through it. With Cal and Richie in the back, Nick looking on, Richie started some kind of lecture with him like he had with Nick the other night. He didn't look too hot to do it but with Cal stuffing down more food Richie started figuring it was now or never—What do you do for money Cal?—You guys. You know I'm glad you said that Cal, because I've been wondering what you'd do without us? Out on the fuckin' road man, Cal pointing out the window. I always meant to say, you're a couple of far-fuckin'-out people, you too Nick, old Nick, he's my sidekick, I remember him back when we was in Thunder Bay, standin' by the road in the hot sun and all that good kinda shit, fuck Nick I was always gonna ask ya, how come you went walkin' down the road that way after we got picked up the first time, I knew we was gonna get picked up, I was even gonna tell ya when if you'd stuck around, I got all kindsa good Karma I brung from California—Nick turning away because he couldn't stand to look Cal in the eye—Richie saying far-fuckin'-out I didn't know you guys were together, what did you split up for Nick—You should know how to dig that right off Richie if you had any kind of Karma cause the whole trip is Nick had only himself to blame for not sticking with me when I had the Karma to know when we were gonna get picked up cause all alone back at that intersection Nick you mighta not had enough Karma to make it on your own. Together we could have tripped out, but that was the chance you took bein' by yourself with only your own Karma thing you dig? What if you didn't get a ride? The only thing that saved you was luck. That's right said Ted, we might not have picked you up, Nick turning red wanting to pull his high-school jacket back over his head like before. Why was he the only one in the truck who couldn't say smart things? By this time he was the one who'd better start doing some talking but he couldn't even look smart, saying to Ted we must be running low on gas why don't we get it filled, thinking I gotta do something to shut them up, Ted saying we're doing fine, Nick trying not to listen to Richie tell Cal he was hip to all the hassles going down on him but how did he feel about living off of other people's money and taking their food like he was doing here. Cal just gave him the high-sign and said it was a stoned gas and a groove, and what did it to him most was people who knew where his head was at, just makin' it his own way and anybody who could dig it like Ted or Richie could lay bread on him and be his stoned brothers—Oh wowww said Richie embracing Cal, too much, Cal saying yeah he just grooved his own way and anybody who could lay bread on him for his trip could be a part of it cause he was sick of these hung-up people all hung up on their material selves were so fucked-up in the head he couldn't stand it and really the main trip about his whole trip was that he dug that he had to do his thing for the straight people, every time he did something it was for the straight people, if it was out on the road for them, sweatin' for them, ballin' for them, panhandlin' for them, just groovin' for 'em somehow he knew that just himself doin' all these outasight things will make it less of a hassle for them in life. Richie couldn't say anything but Oh wowww, Ted kept driving and Cal said I have to take an awful leak, could you gimme 50¢ for a milkshake and stop at this gas station, Richie handing over the money and going oh woww what a beautiful person for five minutes while Cal had his milkshake and piss, Ted climbing out of the driver's seat for Richie. Baby-Face sat up front with Richie, Ted and Nick silent in the back, thinking there was nothing more he could do, Cal had these guys eating out of his hand he might as well admit it, whatever Cal wanted these guys were going along with. The road continued to swoop down over the prairies, the end of Saskatchewan in sight. At some places hitch-hikers went by like telephone poles, getting a roasting from the sun. Nick could almost hear the sound of empty canteens clinking at their sides. He closed his eyes and gritted his teeth. He had to hang on with these guys no matter what, if they let him—if Cal let him. Nick was beginning to think Cal was a better man than him. If he had to go out on the road again he might die, seeing a few bodies lying motionless by the shoulder a while back, not even a subway stop in between anywhere. Nick suddenly wanted to tell them he was sorry for everything, all the trouble he'd caused.

What's wrong Nick, looks like you've got claustrophobia, feel closed in by the wide open spaces, Nick saying I'm OK where I am thanks. Ted throwing banana peels out the window, I can't wait to come up here and get away from it all. I feel as if it's virgin territory up here, you could really get into making money if you came up with a package that would enable you to exploit the fact that they don't have up here what you're trying to sell— This is Swift Current up here said Richie, Cal saying I need a quarter for a coke, let's stop at this gas station. Richie handed over the money as they pulled up, sitting down in back of Ted after Cal jumped out and ran for a coke machine. Yeh, I was wondering, what kind of job do you have in Toronto Nick, any plans for a career—Nick saying he was a load-order despatcher, best thing he could think of off the top of his head, $150 a week. Oh. We were wondering since we're both being drafted in the States and considering moving to Canada and I wonder if you could give us any advice about the employment situation. Both of us just graduated from Princeton. We spoke to some anti-draft organization and they said don't bother coming up because there's no jobs but there must be *something*, where would be a good place to look? Nick said if he knew where he'd go there himself, I read in the papers that people who are worst off have university degrees, sounds like they aren't worth the paper they're printed on anymore—Now wait a minute, Ted turning around, I didn't go to some school in the sticks up here, what do you know—What did you ask me for if you think I don't know anything—Well just because you're an anti-intellectual slob doesn't mean we have to treat you like one—Is that right? well maybe I'll see you back in TO pumping gas, Ted getting out of the driver's seat so he could actually see what Nick was saying—Look at you you're just another stupid blue-collar pig, all you want is a job—No stupider than you for putting up with some freak who sponges off us all the time—You can't say that about Cal, he's a true outlaw in his time, if you had half the creativity he had to be so beautiful we wouldn't mind having you along—Is that right, well I don't like having that damn sponge sponge off me, Nick picking up Cal's gear and throwing it out the back door. He got it stuck open and in the confusion Ted took his laundry bag and threw it out before he could do anything. Nick leaped out the back door to get it Ted slammed the door behind him, Nick panicking, running back pounding on the door yelling yah going to Vancouver or what, gimme a ride—almost jumping on the bumper but it slipped out from under him and he was left lying on the road with his and Cal's clothes scattered down the highway.

THE YEAR

Nora Keeling

Then they lowered the long box that contained her into the ground. The sun made the knobs on it shine and blink. There were a lot of people standing around, and I bumped into one, a fat female relative, and I remember that I spoke to her briefly of the relationship between obesity and longevity. She appeared to be dazed. The sun was glaring directly into her eyes, and she closed them quickly for a moment. When they opened I saw a small tear squeeze out of one of them. I wondered if it were the effect of the sun or of grief. Then I walked away because I had run out of conversation.

The head of the department had given me a three days' leave of absence. I took a week and a day, because Thanksgiving happened to be on a Monday, nor did I explain myself to him. He accepted it without asking for an explanation. His largesse surprised me. Most faculty chairmen aren't so generous. For a long time after that, when I should have been preparing lessons, I sat and gazed ahead of me.

I thought of the evening of the funeral, when I had taken my son to a livestock auction. He was two years old at the time and he laughed and clapped and threw chunks of food as each animal was prodded into the arena. And the sound of the auctioneer's gavel as it hit the altar-like box behind which he sat, his pebbly and interminable voice, seemed oddly to delight the boy. The auctioneer, a big, pink man, looked over at us frequently on the highest tier where we sat, and from which our legs dangled without reaching to the row below. He smiled until his face was crinkled out of shape, like used gift-wrapping. My small son was so delighted by the whole performance that I finally laughed at his laughter. There were other people dispersed throughout the theatre who knew us well and they had long faces. Most of them had narrowed their eyes to fasten them on me, until one of them, heavy-lidded, took on the mask of a reptile. I found their behaviour impolite. They ought to have been watching the sale.

Outside my office in the *sous-sol* the trees were changing colour. Their thick trunks disappeared into the ground. I could imagine their old roots, insolently alive, shooting out into every direction, burrowing deeper and deeper into the earth so they would miss the cold of winter and continue to suck, without gratitude, from their brown surroundings.

Four months ago the leaves had still been broad and green and filled with juices. We had all been at the lake and I had insisted that she let me photograph her. She had refused. She didn't like to have her picture taken, so that, in the end, I took a photograph of her when she wasn't looking. Later I put it in my album. I was pleased with it. She was standing on the shore with one foot in the water and the other out, scooping up shovelfuls of sand for my little boy. Her feet were bare and small and she wore a blue dress with white polka dots on it. She had hoisted up her skirt so that her legs showed. They were still slim and small drops of water rolled down them. Her face was in profile and so was my son's. The lake sparkled under the sun and she was squinting so that her face, with its wide nose, looked comic. Laugh wrinkles made little creases at each side of it, and her pale hair was unruly in the wind.

I wished that classes might end so that I could go home and shut the shades and the drapes and then sit at the kitchen table where I would look at the photograph. But I still had two hours to spend in this institutional, green-coloured office with its big windows that looked out on the parched foliage of a row of maples.

I remembered that I had sent a copy of the photograph

to her with a message. I said she ought be glad that I had taken it. Some day her grandchildren would look at it, and somebody would remark on it. "There's your grandmother," they would say. And the children would laugh, as she had, and not quite believe it and go back to their swings and their tree-climbing, oblivious to the dark roots that would be feeding beneath them. And they wouldn't really care very much. Children should be happy people most of the time. I wondered if they were.

A few weeks after the grotesque ceremony I acquired a photograph of her when she was a girl of eighteen. She had had bobbed hair and light eyes. I put it on my son's wall, beside a row of other photos, because I didn't want it in my own room. One evening I took a picture of him, sitting up in his bed holding a stuffed animal, forgetting that her picture was behind him, just to his left. When the prints came back to me the picture of her was unreal, for it had a curious lighting effect about it, and the face appeared only vaguely through the light, unlike the other photographs on the wall. A religious person might have read something into the result. I'm not one of them, however, as far as I know, and I placed that picture too, into my album, behind the other one.

The days continued to file past me like dreary bipeds in some sort of ritualistic procession. The leaves on the trees finished drying out and dropped. Winter would come soon and the ground would freeze and solidify. When it did, I visited the house in the north where she had lived. I sat at the table where we used to sit and I could feel her looking at me and I could hear her speaking. Sometimes she would sigh and that would annoy me, and then I would feel guilty for having been so angry, and that would make me angrier still. I would see her face. Her eyes were too blue. At times, if the light were right, they were just an ordinary blue. They looked intently at people. When I was feeling irrational I imagined that she could guess what I was thinking, and I would turn away from them.

I left after a few hours because the house was chilly and snow-flakes began to film over the trees and the ground where she was, not far from where I had been sitting.

I went back only once after that. It was the following spring. I tried to visit the cemetery and as I travelled toward it I thought that I would have to walk over the warm ground that covered the box. So I didn't arrive, for I had begun to wonder what would have happened to the obscene flower they had pinned onto her blue dress, and what further would happen when summer came. So that I didn't know anymore which of the seasons of the year I hated most nor which I most feared.

At night when I was in my big bed, and when I had shut the blinds and the drapes so that I could neither see nor hear people treading outside on the ground below, oblivious to what was beneath them, and when I could no longer feel the summer and when I was finally forgetful and almost asleep, I would hear the telephone ring, and I would leap up to answer it, knowing that it was she. She would apologize for not having written for so long. I would do the same. I liked her voice, pitched low and always consistent with itself. I guess other people would have found it ordinary. And I would explain about the birthday present that I had picked for her so carelessly, that had arrived the day after she had been buried, and I would explain why I had been away for so long, and why I had written to her so seldom, why the letters had been so lazy and trite, and I would render a full account of myself and perhaps she would listen, and she would know then that it had been intolerable and that I was happy that it was over.

THE MILL

Andreas Schroeder

What little light is left after sunset reflects weakly in the rear-view mirror. The man driving leans toward the dash, flicks on the lights and settles back into his seat, replacing his grip on the steering-wheel. He murmurs an atonal, irritated tune, unconsciously at determined variance with the droning of the tires on the road.

Hmm . . . mmmm . . . hmhmhm . . . mmm . . . mm . . . hmhm . . . mmmmm . . . hm.

As the darkness settles more firmly into the bushes along the pavement, the car begins steadily to fade, to lose its shape until eventually it is reduced to nothing but its sharply-glaring headlights, pushing their stiff white funnels through the black. Behind these lights the vehicle hangs attached to its feelers like the bone-plated brain behind the driver's eyes, into which the details of the road feed smoothly and continuously as the car proceeds. The driver continues to murmur his tune.

Hmm . . . mmmm . . . hmhmhm . . . mmm . . . mm . . . hmhm . . . mmmm . . . hm.

Lit without warning, trees rear abruptly into the unnatural white, glowing a startled silver; clumps of rock and dirt-piles seem suddenly arrested in the process of scattering, and the broken white line along the pavement clicks by with an almost audible regularity.

Tick . . . tick . . . tick . . . tick . . . tick . . . tick. . . .

The clock on the dash indicates just past eight o'clock. Evening, sunset and the last light are totally erased. To the man at the wheel it seems as if there has never been anything but the darkness.

Behind the dash, the several tiny coloured lights glimmer faintly like embers through cracks between various dials and grilles, scribbling irrational little rainbow patterns on levers and protruding buttons. The only discernible movement is the irresolute back-and-forth rolling of the steering-wheel under the partially visible hands of the driving man. As his hands shuttle through the soft rays of light, fingers appear and disappear as if reacting to an incredibly increased rate of growth and decay.

Behind the wheel, the man appears only in small pieces, an incomplete puzzle whose missing sections are invisible because they seem unwilling to reflect what little light there is. As he shifts slightly with the movements of the car, the underside of his face comes occasionally into view; and his eyes, guttering faintly among the face's shadows.

Ahead, the road abruptly veers from the light and is gone. One of the hands disappears toward the floor of the car, the engine whine increases momentarily as the transmission is levered into a lower gear and the motor adjusts to its new load. The car slows, then turns with the road to the left.

As the unseen foot forces the accelerator toward the floor and the car urges forward through a series of badly-banked and gravel-strewn curves, an uneven orange glow of light appears among the trees a short distance ahead. In response, the man's face approaches the windshield inquiringly for a moment, then retreats. The brief glimpse of his forehead reveals a criss-cross of deeply-scored lines across the skin, like the confused tangle of fallen timber on the logged face of a hill.

The car clears the curves and hurries down a straight stretch, now bearing almost directly toward the increasing light. As it nears the last shield of trees, the driver's complete face becomes visible more often against the glass. Around his mouth and eyes the lines are bunched in expressions of irritation or confusion, the eyes half-smouldering under reddened lids and partially closed.

Badly-shaven cheeks untidy his face and give it a worn-out look. From certain angles, when the glass reflects the growing light more directly, small beads of sweat cling to his forehead and brows.

Soon the entire front end of the car reappears behind its lights, the chrome gleaming softly in the uneasy luminescence. Trees increase in detail, their leaves a flickering of nervous compass needles through uncertain dark. Up ahead, the road banks away to the right, its holes and patches now clearly visible. The car enters the curve and slows.

Beside the road, grotesquely highlighted by its own flames, a sawmill stands on pilings, burning.

The man stops his car and gets out.

A gust of wind carries a scattering of sparks over his head and away into the dark. Across the road the faint crackling of burning timbers reaches him sporadically with the constantly shifting breeze. The sawmill's outer walls stand overgrown with a dancing, hissing ivy of flames.

A blazing timber wavers, then tumbles, outbursting sparks. Spitting embers explode through the air in bristling parabolas, subsiding slowly, darkening toward the ground. Around the spot, flames leap urgently for some moments, then settle back to a steady, flickering burn.

To the man, who realizes he has arrived too late to feel responsible for any attempts at rescue, the scene seems for a short while almost peaceful.

Briefly, watching the flames laughing among the wood, the man forgets even his own troubles.

Yet after those first moments of unmixed enjoyment, uneasiness resettles in his face, an uneasiness of conscience; about permitting the unacceptable to proceed unchallenged; about surreptitiously throwing in his lot with an incendiary force he has no right to entertain, being a man depending on the co-operation of his own consciousness to survive.

He has been taught to confront such events as disasters.

In an almost dutiful attempt at rationalizing, he undertakes to explain his fascination with the flames. What he is seeing, after all, is only an unusually beautiful speeded-up rate of growth and decay running its course in answer to some prior irregularity elsewhere; no man can be blamed for witnessing rather than fighting such an event.

Standing by the side of the road, his arm resting on the door-frame of his car, the man watches the mill disintegrate.

And yet, despite the magnificence of the flames, he feels the fear will come. What he is at present determined to view as an entertainment, a brilliant staging in which the disastrous consequences only serve to heighten his fascination, will at the last moment leap the fire-break, will force his instinctive defence of a world he no longer intends to believe, will refuse his blessing and oblige him to retrench where creation and destruction are incompatible within a single brain.

He stands now tensely, watching himself watching himself watching.

Already, as the pain in his head increases, he begins lamely to reason that a destruction of such magnitude really should be discussed with others, should be analyzed and even possibly adjusted. Helplessly, aware he is recognizing the danger of witnessing such a fire alone, he begins to babble into the darkness, into the ears that must be there, attached to those people who always gather around disintegrating ruins.

It is then that he realizes he has not seen another person anywhere.

This seems unlikely. A fire of such size might easily spread, extending itself beyond all hope of control. Pulling on a jacket, he pushes the car door closed, locks it and begins slowly to circle the mill in search of the people he feels must be there.

He finds no-one. Nor is there any fire-fighting equipment of any consequence anywhere in evidence. A few scattered water-pails in the vicinity of what must have been the office. Above the main mill entrance, two high-voltage spotlights glare blindly across the wide, steel-rimmed gates, their illuminating power rendered virtually useless by the brightness of the flames.

Eventually, floundering unsteadily through the mud behind the mill, the man discovers buildings not yet touched; a small company-town to all appearances. One of the first large sheds he reaches is the fire-hall, its windows totally dark. He presses his face against the grimy glass. The engine stands inside, locked in and unattended. There is no fire-alarm box in sight.

The man looks irresolutely up and down the street. Several houses have lighted windows and several chimneys are blowing smoke. He starts for the nearest house hesitantly, wavering between his antagonism and his need for others, between his responsibility to help other men and his desire to secure their help exclusively for himself. Even here he can feel a faint heat from the distant flames, drifting in slow waves along the street.

The first house is empty.

He stares uncomprehending at the logs burning in the dining-room grate, the switched-on television in the living-room and the partially-eaten food on the kitchen table. No-one answers his calls. The neighbouring house proves to be as empty as the first.

An increasingly frenzied search of the entire town simply emphasizes what he discovered at the beginning. There is no other person anywhere.

It begins to dawn on the man that the fire may have leaped its boundaries in ways considerably more complex than he has been prepared for. He suspects, now, that even if the town was full of people, he may not have been in any position to recognize them.

Back at the mill, he leans a shaking arm against one of the gate-posts and watches the flames toss about.

A muffled explosion somewhere in the middle of the collapsing mill sends multiple fingers of hissing sparks into the air, like jets from an artesian well. A shingled roof hesitates, then slides from its supports, flinging cascades of flaming shakes across the ground. Smoke billows and fades. . . .

The man lifts his head, the cold sweat now clearly visible as it trickles down his cheeks and nose. Hooking into the wire fencing of the gate with both hands, he pulls himself jerkily along its length to an overturned oil drum to sit down. There he leans against the wire, letting his arms drop with an exhausted sigh. Through the irises of his eyes, the flames twist and flutter like the wings of a crippled bird.

As he gazes into the fire, the most difficult thing for the man to grasp is that it probably doesn't exist. In a time of highly-developed and easily-accessible lines of communication, of sophisticated fire-fighting techniques and widespread insurance covering virtually every form of disaster, such unattended fires, such completely abandoned towns in a densely-populated country simply do not occur. Watching a heavy plank platform collapsing into the flames, the man realizes this, but he also realizes now that he is too weak to make the return journey to his car, that he has nothing left to keep him alive but the warmth of this fire.

He knows, too, that the company town will soon begin to burn as well, extending his means of survival a little further.

And he anticipates, lastly, a few final hours keeping alive huddled over the fitfully burning limbs of his own body.

THE MAN WHO KILLED HEMINGWAY

Gail Fox

The room held everything I valued: a typewriter, my notes and poems, a few records of Beethoven and my record player. Also, some old books, which I didn't read so I could concentrate on my writing. I had moved in at the end of April. By the first week in May, my typewriter had been stolen, and the police had come and told me that I belonged back in the hospital. Then one of them asked: "Did you really have a typewriter, or *did you just imagine it*?" I had no defences and began to cry. My handwriting was such that I knew I could never read my poems if written out. I had no money. The police were useless and cruel. I felt my limited resources draining away before a cold and efficient and dishonest world. The cop's pen clicked in my mind for the next few weeks. It sounded like a key in a lock and the lock held back my spirit like a door, a far stronger door than I could afford.

So I listened to Beethoven. I had bought his string trios at a better time, and had held on to them although my fortunes had fallen from a low ebb to an even lower ebb when I became sick. In the hospital, to listen to Beethoven was to be mad. Here, Beethoven was the only sanity. I listened all day and late into the night wondering what I would do next. I had a job, but rarely showed up. It was a waitressing job with a group of very alienated people. They cared nothing about me and I knew that when I didn't come in twice or three times a week, they didn't miss me or even wonder why. They were grey in colour. People had colours at this time. I was blue-purple—a boy in the hospital told me that this was so.

"You have a blue-purple colour and a blue-purple aura and it's beautiful."

His eyes were very bright, he saw auras, he hallucinated, he had visions of Christ. But I wasn't interested in my aura.

"What is the colour of Beethoven's aura?"

His eyes were very bright, I tried to see into them to discover the answer.

"I don't know who that is," he said. And I was sad. And he was sad and never talked to me again.

But listening to Beethoven in the room with the broken door was comforting. Beethoven somehow strengthened the door, bolted it with strong and vibrant strips of melody. I felt hopeful, safe, almost beautiful when I listened to Beethoven. My appearance at this time was quite off-putting. I felt on the few occasions when I left the room to go out that people stared at me as I passed them. I was probably less paranoid than I thought, later. But any kind of madness is relative. In a room with Beethoven, I was beautiful and no-one stared at my uncombed hair, and no-one listened. Until I met Joe.

Joe lived next door and looked like a piece of soft string. His colour was white (whether or not his aura was white I never found out). He looked haunted as if his dreams were horrible and followed him. He wanted to be a writer too. The first day I met him he was in blue jeans and no shirt. His chest was caved in like an accident. I stared at it so long that I felt obliged to tell him I had just gotten out of the hospital—to make us more equal. He was very sympathetic, and when he smiled I saw that many of his teeth were missing. How could that be, I wondered. He was only slightly older than I, and I was young, almost a child.

And then he frowned. "I often think I'm mad, too. I live a very private life and the things I write have meaning one day and not the next."

I wasn't sure of his madness, I was sure of his friendship. We drank some wine from his refrigerator, and it wasn't until some days later that I realized that all he had in his refrigerator was wine. He was my first friend out of the hospital. His room was rather like a hospital room. A single hard bed. A side table with a rickety lamp. A heavy Victorian chest of drawers. No rug on the floor, no picture on the wall. The refrigerator stood in front of the only window. I was curious about him but wisely decided not to ask any questions. Instead I told him about my job, and the stolen typewriter, and the sneering callous attitude of the police, and lots of things. In fact, I talked for hours. And then I didn't see him until a few days later for a drink, and then I didn't see him for a week. During this time, I listened to Beethoven and bought some lipstick at a Negro dimestore nearby. The lipstick colour was Shocking Red, the only kind they carried, and I wore it like a disguise.

One day, I sat in my room and Joe knocked. I got up to let him in, but something told me not to open the door. "Yes?" I said.

"It's happened," he said softly. His voice was blurred. Then curiously, I slid open the door and he half fell into the room, hard down on one knee. His jacket was torn and his right arm was covered with blood. I was very frightened and didn't know what to do.

"Were you in a fight?" I asked, hesitating as I noticed the blood dropping like kidney beans on the floor in front of the door.

"Christ." He wiped his arm over his face. Blood smeared his eyes and he had to blink as he looked at me. I must have looked ghastly too.

"Promise you won't tell anyone."

"Of course."

Trying to guess what he would tell me. A bar fight? But he didn't go to bars. An accident? Probably an accident. He was so clumsy. He moved like an accident. None of his bones seemed to do anything. They were lost somewhere deep in the private flesh even he knew nothing about.

"All right," he said. "I just killed a man."

No. I didn't believe it and I told him I didn't and I

laughed. And then before he could interrupt me, I told him a long story about Hemingway and how he used to fight in the bars of Spain, and how he nearly killed several men, but never actually succeeded.

"That's funny," he said. The blood was forming intricate flowers on the floor. "That's funny. The guy I killed tonight was Hemingway."

I couldn't think of anything but the ridiculous. "Do the police know?"

"Yes."

Immediately, I panicked. I couldn't have the police again. They would ask me if my typewriter had reappeared, and laugh and say: "How are you feeling these days, lady?" So. Quietly. I told Joe to go back into his room and lie down. But first, I wrapped part of a sheet around his arm at a pressure point, remembering vaguely a first-aid class in high school, and a teacher who wore skirts to her calves. Grey skirts. Another grey person.

"Let's go, Joe," I said, and he got out his key, left-handed, and opened the adjoining door. It was later that I first saw his writing.

He told me to reach into the first drawer of his bureau. I felt darkness, then a few pages of rough typing paper. "That's it," he said.

There were about twenty pages, odd, white, like everything about him. "This is my best story," he said softly. The story was called "The Killers." I didn't think until years later that Hemingway had written a story of the same name. But Joe's story was full of an argot I didn't connect with Hemingway. Words like *pimp, queen, trick*; about boys who did it with boys, and girls who did it with girls. I was very embarrassed. Also conscious that soon the police would come and we wouldn't look scared or concerned or even penitent. We would merely be sitting in Joe's room, looking at his strange story. So I decided to go back to my room, but leave my door unlocked so that Joe could say goodbye when the police took him away. I went back and went to sleep and didn't wake until the next morning.

The next morning. I crawled out of bed thinking

vaguely that something was terribly wrong. My head was thick as if I had drunk too much of Joe's wine, and then I thought, Joe! I dressed and ran to his door. It was locked. But every now and then I could hear a low voice muttering as if from a dream.

I went back to my room. And quickly, my thoughts were as follows: He didn't kill Hemingway. He didn't kill anyone. Maybe he killed Hemingway, but I'm his friend so he wouldn't kill me.

Then I put on Beethoven and listened to my heart beat against my head. All my writing in the next few days was distracted by Joe's blood on the floor. It wouldn't come up. I tried to read what I wrote, but I couldn't. My hands shook.

I didn't want to see Joe. I knew he was there and occasionally I heard him go out for wine and then return. He never attempted to see me either, which was fortunate. I was feeling on the verge of something bad, something like another breakdown, or an acute sense of anomie. I thought of suicide increasingly, and for that reason decided to go back to work on a regular basis. My fellow workers didn't even raise an eyebrow when I came in after a three weeks' absence. My boss handed me an envelope with the deductions written on the back and mumbled something about "you can't get it for nothing, you know." At this point, I did nothing, I expected nothing. And even that slim envelope helped.

Increasingly, however, I was behind in rent, and one day came back to find the landlord beating on the door. Practically beating it down, it seemed.

"Here I am," I said, stepping forward in the dim light so he could see me. He glanced vacantly at me, and then back at the door.

"It's you. I thought you'd run away."

I must have looked rather bewildered. Then he said: "When I saw *them* out in the car, I thought you was with them."

Since I didn't know anyone but Joe, I was even more puzzled. "I'm sorry," I said awkwardly. "I don't know who you mean."

He pulled himself up to his full height, which was shorter than me, and suddenly a mouse appeared out of nowhere. He grimaced. "You're forcing me to say that word and I don't like it. I can tell you that."

He looked so mad and shy and inept that I began to feel sorry for him, and tried to help him out. "I don't know anyone but Joe who lives here," and I motioned toward the locked door behind him.

"Well."

He didn't believe me, I could tell. His eyes were small and screwed into knots.

"I'll just tell you this—I don't want to see you with no lesbian-butches. I'll tell you that. Gives my place a bad name."

He spat out the words like bad food and, mouselike, I longed to run away, to disappear into the hole that was the dirty hall. Finally, he left. I didn't remember what he had said until I closed the door on him. Then only two things occurred to me: that he hadn't said anything about the rent, and that once Joe had told me that his best friends were a couple of girls who lived together, and who, he claimed, would really like me.

I felt frightened and decided to get into bed. Just as I undressed, I saw a car drive up with a heavy girl at the wheel. I knew without anyone telling me that this was Elizabeth, one of Joe's friends.

I was so certain that she was coming to see me, that I turned off all the lights and double-locked the door. Then I pulled on my clothes and hid behind a chair near the door, so that if she looked through the keyhole she would see no-one. I was shaking. It was so hard for me to get along with people, let alone Elizabeth—if the landlord was right, of course. But of course he was. Things like this don't stay hidden, they get out, they expand, they take over. I crouched behind the chair and focused on some of Joe's blood remaining on the floor. It was the colour of dark liver now and had lost its smell.

Then I heard Elizabeth coming up. Just when I thought I would scream, I heard her knock at Joe's door. I was so relieved, I almost yelled out: "Joe's there, go on in!" And then, as if everything were working out in a way I hadn't planned, I heard Joe's voice, and his door open, and Elizabeth go in. She was laughing.

An hour later, or perhaps it was two hours, I heard Joe's door open again. I was cramped from my rigid position and fear, and as I moved my arm I noticed that it was wet. I had been crying. I was so surprised that I thought of my mother. And the time she hit me with a hairbrush in front of my best friend. I had been so humiliated, I didn't realize I was crying until later in my room. My best friend never mentioned it. She was brain-damaged and may not have realized what was going on. If she had realized, she would have been angry. She reacted that way. But I never got angry. I was passive and tolerant to the point of nausea.

When Joe's door opened again, I only wanted to sleep. And strange thoughts went through my head like "If I move to the left, I could grab the scissors and do it before anyone would know." Thoughts like that. I heard talking and then someone going downstairs. Suddenly, Joe yelled:

"Melinda, are you there?"

I was so startled, I blurted out "Yes!" coming in like a violin on cue, O Beethoven, so perfect I hated myself. "Now's the time," I thought, "now's the time."

"Melinda!"

He was rattling the door and sounded upset. I didn't want to see him, I didn't want to have anything to do with him again. And yet, I found myself getting up and opening the door. I opened the door without looking at him. He came in, dragging his body like a flat tire. I sensed this. He was like such a familiar nightmare. I must have looked haunted myself, as if *my* dreams followed *me* (which they did).

"Melinda! Thank God you're here! I've gotten this girl pregnant and I've got to find someone who can fix it. She doesn't want the child and God knows, I don't."

I looked at him then and he looked as if his words were not connected to him. He looked calm and white and drunk but somehow strong. He was looking at my lipstick and saying:

"Nigger lipstick. That's all you get."

That made me angry. For the first time in two years, I was angry. Instead of being passive and waiting for myself to puke, I said:

"Joe, I want you to tell me what's happening. I don't understand. You're crazy, you're unreal—is it Elizabeth's baby? I want to know these things, or I can't be your friend!"

By now I was shouting. I was as loud as Beethoven storming at the furies in his head. Joe looked at me. His eyes blinked a couple of times like traffic lights, and he muttered something, stopped, and then muttered something again.

"Joe—" I reached for the door, "tell me or get the hell out!"

Then I noticed that his arm was still bandaged with the piece of sheet I had put on two weeks ago. It was dirty, foul and unravelling at both ends. I felt sorry for him.

"Joe," I said it pleadingly.

"All right." He sat down, blinking.

"You must have thought I killed someone the other night."

He wanted me to agree, so I agreed the way I always do.

"Well." His face became suddenly cruel. "I killed Hemingway."

Again I said what he wanted. "That's terrible, Joe."

"Yes." He watched me carefully. "I cut him right through the gut with a knife and then through the neck with a piece of broken bottle. Blood, o lots of blood! Hemingway tried to get me, too, but only managed to scrape up my arm a bit. He was tough." He hesitated, and then leaned forward. "I loved him."

"That's terrible, Joe," I said automatically. I sounded like an iceberg.

Joe sprang up defensively. "It's not terrible! It's beautiful. It's like drinking or dreaming, like Elizabeth and Anne, all my friends, everyone. And you say 'it's terrible, Joe!' You bitch!" He began to weep.

I didn't say anything. I ran out. I ran to a small bar on Orange Street and rammed myself and all my twisted feelings into a phone booth.

"Hello. Mother, I just wanted to tell you that I want to come home. No, nothing's wrong. Everything's just fine. No, I'm not crying. I'm just out of breath. Yes, I really want to stay but I'm out of money. OK. See you."

I stayed until it was dark, drinking among the students, who paid me no attention because I was so clearly not one of them. The music was unfamiliar and everyone was singing along. I drank and drank. At twelve, I got up and found I couldn't walk. So I crawled the last two blocks on my knees. It was weird, it was holy. It was the last time.

Mother arrived promptly at ten. That's when she had said she would. She was bustling and cheerful and horrified at everything. She was horrified at the room and the way the door leaned in. She lectured me about my typewriter and said that I'd never learn. She said:

"But the police will come up with something, I'm sure. They're so helpful, *don't you think?*"

She gave me a long look. By now I wasn't saying anything. Just putting things in boxes, running around, thinking that the worst thing that could happen would be for Joe to come in. And then it happened.

"Open the door," said Mother. "Maybe it's one of your friends to say goodbye."

"No, it's, it's no-one," I stammered. "I mean it's just someone who drinks a lot I never like to see."

"Well, you never know," said Mother. And clicking over, she opened the door. There stood Joe, terribly white, drunk and calm. Mother took one look at him and then said sweetly:

"Is this *Joe*, your *best* friend?"

It was obvious that it was Joe. He was wearing a round button on his shirt with JOE printed on it in large Old-English letters. He said nothing, just stared as Mother reproved him with her eyes, her hands, her grey skirt, even the way her hair was parted. Then she started talking in a busy way, ignoring everything—telling me what to take and what to leave behind.

"These old sweaters—you don't need these at home. And what's this? Beethoven string trios, hmm. Pretty gloomy stuff for you."

She threw them into a pile of discarded newspapers. "Got to keep my daughter cheerful, right Melinda?" She seemed to be addressing Joe. Joe just stood there.

Then he turned to me and said without a trace of expression: "So this is the abortionist I asked you to find. She's pretty skilful." And he went out, quietly closing the door.

Strangely enough, I found myself laughing, hysterically, but laughing.

"Don't mind him, Mother. He's just the guy who lives next door who drinks too much. He used to be a circus clown, then he scratched his arm and now he drinks. He tried to make me pregnant once, and now I am. I'm pregnant, Mother! It's good you came along. Here's my hairbrush!"

Mother looked a bit startled. And then she took the hairbrush and threw it into the pile of discarded things. "I guess that's all," she said. She stepped toward the door clicking like a pair of castanets. When she came to Joe's blood, she said:

"You spilled some spaghetti on the floor, Melinda. Shall I wipe it up?"

"No," I said through my teeth.

And then Mother laughed. "Don't worry, everything will be all right. And Father can hardly wait to see you, he'll be so surprised."

And I laughed too. And I couldn't believe in myself or Joe or Elizabeth or Hemingway or Mother. And I just stood there laughing and wondering where Mother had put the scissors by now.

WHO CAN AVOID A PLACE?

David McFadden

It must have been 90. It was one hot day in late spring and it made Brownie wonder how he could have failed to appreciate the period of cool weather just past.

Brownie was walking east on the north side of King Street, between Catharine and Mary streets, and the three or four dominant parts of his brain were quietly rehashing stale arguments:

Eat at Oval's. Nah, eat at Funland, more fun. No, Funland won't be open yet. Don't eat at all, fast till five. It's too hot to eat. Oval's will be cool. For regularity eat regularly.

The sun was hot, brain was stale and underneath it all Brownie slipped his watch off his left wrist and slipped it into his pocket for coolness. In hot weather pay attention to the wrists, keep them cool. Hold an ice cube between your wrists and the fever fades. And underneath it all Brownie sang obsessively (to himself):

> *I don't care if it boils or freezes*
> *Because I'm safe in the arms of Jesus. . . .*

King Street traffic was all bottled up at Mary Street. Three miserably hot and begrimed workmen stood in the middle of the intersection boiling and pouring tar and asphalt, one big bear of a workman and two smaller guys. The smoke and fumes gushed into the air and thinned out in numerous directions. Traffic crept around both sides of the work area and cautiously through the billowing white smoke of tar. The sentimental smell of boiling tar.

It was too strong to be sentimental yet too sentimental to be obnoxious and too hot to think about. Why did Brownie think all the time? When it was so definitely no matter of enjoyment. Obsession, that's what it was. If you're not thinking all the time you might miss something. Some great ideas. Then why not enjoy it? *Click*.

Brownie pushed open the door and walked into Oval's. Coooool air, ahhh! About twenty stools along the long counter. About fourteen occupied. Had Brownie at last found his true occupation? A stool-counter? *Ooops!* Behind the counter that goddamned stupid miserable money-grubbing curly-haired Greek with the mouth like a kangaroo's pouch. No, this is Canada. A mouth that reminded Brownie of a miniature Hamilton Harbour. Brownie had forgotten about him. And now here he was. And here was Brownie.

Brownie had forgotten he was supposed to be avoiding this place. Brownie wondered about his memory lapses, why did they occur when least expected? Brownie had been avoiding this place for about a month since the unpleasantness with this guy. Just as well, who can avoid a *place*? About time these little foolishnesses stopped. Be stern with yourself, Brownie. Probably the guy doesn't remember you anyway. But there was money involved. And this guy, what's his name? We'll call him Oval because that's the name of the place. We'll call him Oval, even though Brownie knew he wasn't the owner of the place, just the lead hand, number one help. And there was money involved. You could look and see Oval watching those twenty stools as he worked, twenty stools, fourteen occupied, and not seeing stools or stool occupants, but just dollar signs and rapid profit-and-loss calculations. But there was money involved, even a quarter guys like Oval would remember forever, a mouth like an elephant's memory.

The unpleasantness, the thing that had been causing Brownie to try to avoid this place, what was it, a matter of principle? *I'll never shop in this place again as long as I live?* Not with Brownie. It was more of a *I'll stay away from this place, who can enjoy a sandwich with that guy around ready to start up the argument again maybe.*

One night a month or so before, round about midnight, Brownie had been munching away slowly on a hamburg and listening to Oval's soft-music mantel radio. Then the news came on and Brownie put a quarter in the juke-box. Brownie selected his musical selections, complicated letter-and-number push-button computations, the wheels turned, the world of music spun around on its solar axis, the needle came down and nothing happened. I mean, the record was playing all right but the sound was turned down so low you couldn't hear anything but a scratchy rumbling and tiny indistinct whine, solo.

Brownie was disappointed, not for the lost quarter but for the non-fulfilment of his musical anticipations. Lunch without music isn't the worst thing in the world but lunch without the music you had set your ear up for was disappointing. Brownie said nothing. But when Oval passed by the next time, Brownie blurted out: "Er, excuse me, could you turn the juke-box up? It's playing but there's no volume."

Oval merely sneered at him and snorted impatiently. *No!* And to Brownie's mild disappointment a mild anger and milder thirst for revenge was added. What should I do? Should I do anything? Nothing? Write a letter to the editor? Storm out without paying or finishing this hamburg? Kick the bloody juke-box in?

Brownie finished his hamburg and was picking up crumbs and tiny shreds of onion with a damp finger when Oval slapped the bill down and walked back to the grill. Here was Brownie's chance. He whipped out his pen and deducted 25¢ from the total of the bill, 95¢, leaving 70¢. He finished off his Coke with a graceful glug, got up and walked with determination to the cash register. He dropped 70¢ into Oval's greasy palm and said: "I've deducted 25¢ because I couldn't hear the juke-box." Lucky I had 70¢ exact change, whew, thought Brownie. The juke-box was still silently spinning.

"What?" said Oval, sharply. "Come on, another quarter," he snorted, his ugly face made uglier with irritation. "I have no time for games."

Brownie walked out.

I better never go in there again, thought Brownie out

on the street. At least I'll always peek in the window first to make sure Oval isn't on duty.

And now this hot day of May, a month or so later. The fateful moment had arrived.

Brownie took his stool like in one of the numberless critical scenes of the timeless drama of the Great West.

Would Oval call a cop?

Would he noisily demand his 25¢?

Would he think it mighty odd that Brownie had dared to return to the place of his crime?

Would he refuse to serve him?

Would he just ignore him, pretend he wasn't there until Brownie would be forced to walk out unserved?

Would he centre him out without mercy?

Would he admire Brownie his courage and high Grecian principles?

Would he learn a true lesson about life in truly great Canada?

The critical point dissolved in the relentless stream of time and moved slowly and unstoppably into the irretrievable past. There was the juke-box. Brownie didn't feel tempted to use it, and the radio was tuned to a Top 40 station, medium volume and thin tone.

Oval was busy manning both the grill and the cash register. Which was more important, mused Brownie. You just can't say, they're inseparable, what stupid questions! A waitress Brownie had never seen before took care of the lunch counter. Oval looked at Brownie without differentiation. Just another customer. Just another dollar sign. He looked at his other customers while busy frying and flipping eggs and quarter-pound ground beef patties golden brown one side fungus green the other, and ringing up cash.

Brownie ordered a toasted Western and Coke. Why of all things a toasted Western on such a hot day? Brownie couldn't answer that one. The waitress was skinny, 40, efficient and virginal. "Would you like your Coke now or later?"

Now, said Brownie who wasn't thirsty or hungry either for that matter. Brownie looked around.

On his left was an empty stool then two women and a man occupying the next three stools and chattering away in raw English accents about all the "soo-pah" things they were going to do when one of them, Brownie wasn't sure which, got his or her first pay.

On his right were two empty stools then two guys in their early twenties smoking Rothmans and watching the street and door. One was wearing a Stan Lee tee-shirt, Spiderman. They butted their cigarettes, paid their bill and went out.

A grey-haired woman, tall and thin, was standing in front of the cash register. She was ordering a sandwich to go, or two sandwiches to go. Brownie hadn't seen her come in. She was with her little boy, about eight. She was maybe 50 and was wearing a flowered sleeveless summer shift. Brownie figured they were going to eat their sandwiches in the park under a shady tree where there would be a bit of a cool breeze. Or perhaps on a fume-enshrouded bench on the stark, sun-boiled sidewalk. Then he noticed the woman's tattoo. Faded, but it looked like "A-327" right at her elbow on the outside of her left arm. Funny, she didn't look Jewish thought Brownie. But then again most Jews of Brownie's acquaintance didn't look Jewish. She would have been in her twenties during the war. Was she self-conscious about her number, did she try to cover it up? Did she have to make agonizing decisions every day about whether to wear a long-sleeved or short-sleeved dress? Of course not, she was probably always as unselfconscious about her number as she appeared to be at the moment. It was something to be proud of, if anything, in a ridiculously sad way. But then there would always be the inevitable suspicions of people wondering bitchily and despairingly what she had to do to survive. That which so many millions refused to do? Or weren't given the chance to do? Brownie could see her being released from the concentration camp at the end of the war. Then his imagination sort of wiped itself out and he got back to his Western. The "7" in the "A-327" was delicately crossed in the German way. She was still alive, was the guy who actually did the tattooing still alive? Did she ever think of him? Did he ever think of her?

Not that longevity in itself is anything to write home about. Ah me.

Bang, the three tar workers from the nearby smoky intersection came in with a bang and sat down space one two three on Brownie's right. They were really dirty, and the one closest to Brownie was big as a wrestler. The other two were skinny and younger. They ordered hamburgs, cheeseburgs and milk and chocolate milk. Brownie wondered if they were going to the washroom and they didn't, just sat there silently groaning with the cool conditioned air. They were probably too tired to wash and too hot to pee. Is this naive? You're darned right it is, no city workers work hard. These guys have probably been in and out of here ten times already today. Or is this just a self-comforting illusion, to think the guys who lay our sewers, lay our roads, build our bridges, dig our tunnels have it easy and are always knocking off for half an hour every five minutes?

The three Britons were still excitedly chirping away. Brownie looked at them. They were an attractive-looking trio. They wore clothes obviously bought in Britain, a small inexpensive shop in an obscure town like Casterbridge, and they radiated an attractive happiness with life. Brownie felt like talking to them. He wanted to say: "Hey, you should have the Western. You probably don't know what a Western is because they don't have them yet in England—hah, you probably thought no-one would notice you're from England, hah—and therefore you probably wouldn't bother asking but really I do suggest the Western, Oval's Western is particularly good and all it really is is a ham omelette between two pieces of delicately-buttered toast." Then Brownie noticed the empty plates in front of them, signifying they'd already eaten. So he just looked, a little smile of welcome on his face. One of the women noticed Brownie watching and smiling and she abruptly looked away as did Brownie.

Brownie sipped his cool Coke, no ice, no straw, just the way Brownie liked it.

It was high noon, and the sun filled this nowhere little hamburg place with colour and significance. If there was one ounce of colour and significance and true reality anywhere in God's grey multi-levelled universe it was here in Oval's, and everywhere. Elsewhere in the world innocent people were being burnt and shot and spat upon and hopeless causes were being died for by the strongest and most beautiful of us. The Apollo Ten was orbiting the moon, only nine miles from the moon's surface at that very moment. Something that had never happened in the Golden Age of Athens, never in Shakespeare's time, yet it was happening in Brownie Banana's time.

Brownie's Western came.

Somebody slipped onto the stool right at Brownie's left. It was the bank manager, but Brownie had never had any business with him so ignored him. Brownie, with vigour unexpected in one with such a poor appetite, salted and peppered his Western then grabbed the ketchup bottle. Real ketchup in a real ketchup bottle, not vinegared down. He snapped off the cap and with exaggerated graceful arcs and neatly-balanced parabolas sauced the ketchup onto the overdone omelette as if he wanted his money's worth. And ate voraciously, feigning hunger. And wondering why. And knowing why. If you have no appetite, pretend you have, and soon you will have. It always works, with other things besides appetite, though really everything in essence boils down to appetite.

Appetite is Everything.

God is Appetite.

The bank manager eyed Brownie with amusement as he waited for his order to be taken.

Sure, and somewhere it was freezing, somewhere someone's living blood was boiling in the lost wind-swept sand-duned sun-boiled desert vastness, hopeless, delirious, far from an oasis. And somewhere there were strange life-forms of anguished intelligence unknown to this solar system. And somewhere there were horrors far beyond the scope of the history of man's imagination.

Brownie remembered his wife. He was supposed to phone home to find out if he had to drive to Brantford this afternoon to pick up the new air-compressor. He drained his glass of Coke, picked up the bill, 95¢, and stepped over to the phone. He dialed his wife's number, his number. Busy. He hung up and dialed again. Nothing, no signal at all. He paid the bill, old Oval accepting the money automatically. Oval wasn't really so bad. If he was such a moneygrubber he would have turned up the juke-box full-blast at request, and encouraged Brownie to put more and more money in it. No, not really, they get a flat rate for placing the juke-box and no matter how often or how seldom it's played they get the same flat rate. But anyway, who knows? Can't a guy be unpleasant without creating hostility?

Brownie walked into the street. Hell, it wasn't that hot.

Brownie walked, and somewhere a boat was going down at high sea. Somewhere someone else was walking a hot street thinking maybe somewhere a boat was going down at high sea. Somewhere or sometime.

A fat woman in her early 60's with two library books in her arm passed Brownie. If she's walking from the library she's walking a long way in this heat carrying those books, thought Brownie. He couldn't see the small book, at least to make out what it was, but the big book was a book of quotations. Whenever Brownie saw someone with a book he always tried to see the title. It was a hobby with him. This woman looked so miserable Brownie shuddered in the heat. It was sad. Wouldn't she have a happier look on her face if she'd had an armful of pornographic literature under her arm? Was she so different from the rest of the species that she should prefer that stupid book of quotations to *I, a Woman*, or even *The Jewel in the Lotus*?

Brownie crossed King Street at Mary, through the smoke and fire of the tar layers. He went to the phone booth, the one in front of Terminal Hotel, but the booth wasn't there. A shock all right! Brownie looked up two or three storeys, as if the phone booth had been lifted above eye level by the shimmering waves of heat. Then Brownie looked from side to side. How many times in his life had Brownie put in a call from this booth that had suddenly moved with no warning some time in the past week?

A discoloured rectangle on the sidewalk marked where the phone-booth had been, so Brownie knew it wasn't his mistake. It had been a double booth and had been there at least twenty years. Many were the hasty explanations Brownie had made from it.

Then Brownie noticed another major change in this beloved section of his beloved city. The Terminal Hotel sign had been taken down and in its place had been erected a splendidly gaudy new electronic neon sign: The Running Pump.

Brownie looked around, across, up and down the street for another booth but couldn't find one. He walked toward Terminal Towers and into that new indoor shopping mall.

Not so little, it contained a supermarket, liquor store, restaurants, drug store, radio station, provincial court and scores of little boutiques. Brownie walked toward a pair of modern push-button pay-phones hanging on the wall between a little shoe boutique and a Dutch restaurant.

A plump, red-faced woman in her 40's was standing there directly between the two phones. She fumbled in her purse for change. She was kind of hogging both phones.

"Oops," said the woman with a smile. "Sorry, I'm not really using both phones." She repositioned herself over to the phone on the left, still looking in her purse for a dime. She was probably thinking of all the Chic Young jokes about women and their crazy messy unorganized purses.

"I didn't really think you were," said Brownie with genuine friendliness. "Although I've seen it done. . . ." He thought that was going to be funny but it didn't come out funny. The woman laughed mildly anyway, to show she knew it was meant to be a joke.

"Ah, there it is," said the woman, holding up a dime between finger and thumb.

"Why didn't you tell me you were looking for the dime?" said Brownie. "I've got a watch."

The woman's shoulders jerked in a small spasm of laughter.

"I mean, I've got a dime you could have had." Brownie added in a soft voice.

The woman's full and puckered lips turned up and her eyes crinkled looking straight into Brownie's.

Back to business, they each started dialing their respective numbers.

Brownie finished dialing first, because those push-button phones are set up just like the adding machine

Brownie used when he worked at the bank a few years ago. And he could dial really fast. The ubiquitous William Burroughs.

But the faster you dialed the longer you had to wait for the connection to register.

The line was busy.

Brownie hung up.

The plump, red-faced woman's line was busy too.

She hung up.

They both tried again.

This time, as before in Oval's, there was no signal at all for Brownie.

The woman's line again was busy.

Brownie just held on to the receiver waiting for some signal, waiting for an end of the blankness.

"Damn, I'll try again later," said the plump, red-faced woman, dropping her dime back into the violent jungle of her inner purse. She walked away with a little smile. Brownie continued holding on to the receiver hoping for some signal. None came. He hung up, sighed, took a deep breath and dialed again. Blank, still no signal.

THE GRAVE OF THE FAMOUS POET

Margaret Atwood

There are a couple of false alarms before we actually get there, towns we pass through that might be it but aren't, uninformative stores and houses edging the road, no signs. Even when we've arrived we aren't sure; we peer out, looking for a name, an advertisement. The bus pauses.

"This has to be it," I say. I have the map.

"Better ask the driver," he says, not believing me.

"Have I ever been wrong?" I say, but I ask the driver anyway. I'm right again and we get off.

We're in a constricted street of grey flat-fronted houses, their white lace curtains pulled closed, walls rising cliff-straight and lawnless from the narrow sidewalk. There are no other people, at least it isn't a tourist trap. I have to eat, we've been travelling all morning, but he wants to find a hotel first, he always needs a home base. Right in front of us there's a building labelled HOTEL. We hesitate outside it, patting down our hair, trying to look acceptable. When he finally grits up the steps with our suitcase the doors are locked. Maybe it's a pub.

Hoping there may be a place farther along, we walk down the hill, following the long stone wall, crossing the road when the sidewalk disappears at the corners. Cars pass us, driving fast as if on their way to somewhere else.

At the bottom of the hill near the beach there's a smattering of shops and a scarred, listing Inn. Radio music and hilarious voices from inside.

"It seems local," I say, pleased.

"What does 'Inn' mean here?" he asks, but I don't know. He goes in to see; then he comes out, dispirited. I'm too tired to think up solutions, I'm scarcely noticing the castle on the hill behind us, the sea.

"No wonder he drank," he says.

"I'll ask," I say, aggrieved: it was his idea, he should do the finding. I try the general store. It's full of people, women mostly, with scarves on their heads and shopping baskets. They say there is no hotel; one woman says her mother has some rooms free though, and she gives me directions while the others gaze pityingly, I'm so obviously a tourist.

The house, when we find it, is eighteenth-century and enormous, a summer residence when the town was fashionable. It offers Bed and Breakfast on a modest sign. We're glad to have something spelled out for us. The door is open, we go into the hall, and the woman emerges from the parlour as if startled; she has a forties bobby-soxer hairdo with curious frontal lobes, only it's grey. She's friendly to us, almost sprightly, and yes, she has a room for us. I ask, in a lowered voice, if she can tell us where the grave is.

"You can almost see it right from the window," she says, smiling—she knew we would ask that—and offers to lend us a book with a map in it of the points of interest, his house and all. She gets the book, scampers up the wide maroon-carpeted staircase to show us our room. It's vast, chill, high-ceilinged, with floral wallpaper and white-painted woodwork; instead of curtains the windows have inside shutters. There are three beds and numerous dressers and cupboards, crowded into the room as if in storage, a chunky bureau blocking the once-palatial fireplace. We say it will be fine.

"The grave is just up the hill, that way," she says, pointing through the window. We can see the tip of a church. "I'm sure you'll enjoy it."

I change into jeans and boots while he opens and closes the drawers of all the pieces of furniture, searching for ambushes or reading matter. He discovers nothing and we set out.

We ignore the church—he once said it was unremarkable—and head for the graveyard. It must rain a lot: ivy invades everything, and the graveyard is lush with uncut grass, succulent and light green. Feet have beaten animal-trail paths among the tombstones. The graves themselves are neatly tended, most of them have the grass clipped and fresh flowers in the tea-strainer-shaped flower holders. There are three old ladies in the graveyard now, sheaves of flowers in their arms, gladioli, chrysanthemums; they are moving among the graves, picking out the old flowers and distributing the new ones impartially, like stewardesses. They take us for granted, neither approaching nor avoiding us: we are strangers and as such part of this landscape.

We find the right grave easily enough; as the book says, it's the only one with a wooden cross instead of a stone. The cross has been recently painted and the grave is planted with a miniature formal-garden arrangement of moss roses and red begonias; the sweet alyssum intended for a border hasn't quite worked. I wonder who planned it, surely it wouldn't have been her. The old ladies have been here and have left a vase, yellowish glassware of the kind once found in cereal boxes, with orange dahlias and spikes of an unknown pink flower. We've brought nothing and have no ceremonies to perform; we muse for an acceptable length of time, then retreat to the scrollworked bench up the hill and sit in the sun, listening to the cows in the field across the road and the murmur of the ladies as they stoop and potter below us, their print dresses fluttering in the easy wind.

"It's not such a bad place," I say.

"But dull," he answers.

We have whatever it was we came for, the rest of the day is our own. After a while we leave the graveyard and stroll back down the main street, holding hands absent-mindedly, looking in the windows of the few shops: an overpriced antique store, a handicrafts place with pottery and Welsh weaving, a nondescript store that sells everything, including girlie joke magazines and copies of his books. In the window, half-hidden among souvenir cups, maps and faded pennants, is a framed photograph of his face, three-quarters profile. We buy a couple of ice-cream bars; they are ancient and soapy.

We reach the bottom of the winding hill and decide to walk along to his house, which we can see, an indistinct white square separated from us by half a mile of rough beach. It's his house all right, it was marked on the map. At first we have no trouble, there's a wide uneven pathway, broken asphalt, the remains or perhaps the beginning of a road. Above us at the edge of the steep leaf-covered cliff, what is left of the castle totters down, slowly, one stone a year. For him, turrets are irresistible. He finds a scrabbly trail, a childrens' entrance up sheer mud.

He goes up sideways, crabwise, digging footholds with the sides of his boots. "Come on!" he shouts down. I'm hesitant but I follow. At the top he reaches his hand to me, but, perpendicular and with the earth beside me, afraid of losing my balance, I avoid it and scramble the last few feet, holding on to roots. In wet weather it would be impossible.

He's ahead, eager to explore. The tunnel through the undergrowth leads to a gap in the castle wall; I follow his sounds, rustlings, the soft thud of his feet. We're in the skeleton of a garden, the beds marked by brick borders now grass-infested, a few rose bushes still attempting to keep order in spite of the aphids, nothing else paying any attention. I bend over a rose, ivory hearted, browning at the edges; I feel like a usurper. He's already out of sight again, hidden by an archway.

I catch up to him in the main courtyard. Everything is crumbling, stairways, ramparts, battlements; so much has fallen it's hard for us to get our bearings, translate this rubbish back into its earlier clear plan.

"That must have been the fireplace," I say, "and that's the main gate. We must have come round from the back." For some reason we speak in whispers; he tosses a fragment of stone and I tell him to be careful.

We go up the remnants of a stairway into the keep. It's almost totally dark; the floors are earth-covered. People must come here though, there's an old sack, an unidentifiable piece of clothing. We don't stay long inside: I'm afraid of getting lost, though it's not likely, and

I would rather be able to see him. I don't like the thought of finding his hand suddenly on me unannounced. Besides, I don't trust the castle, I expect it to thunder down on us at the first loud laugh or false step. But we make it outside safely.

We pass beneath the gateway, its Norman curve still intact. Outside is another, larger courtyard, enclosed by the wall we have seen from outside and broken through; it has trees, recent trees not more than a hundred years old, dark-foliaged as etchings. Someone must come here to cut the grass: it's short, hair-textured. He lies down on it and draws me down beside him and we rest on our elbows, surveying. From the front the castle is more complete, you can see how it could once have been lived in by real people.

He lies down, closing his eyes, raising his hand to shade them from the sun. He's pale and I realize he must be tired too, I've been thinking of my own lack of energy as something he has caused and must therefore be immune from.

"I'd like to have a castle like that," he says. When he admires something he wants to own it. For an instant I pretend that he does have the castle, he's always been here, he has a coffin hidden in the crypt, if I'm not careful I'll be trapped and have to stay with him forever. If I'd had more sleep last night I'd be able to frighten myself this way but as it is I give up and lean back on the grass beside him, looking up at the trees as their branches move in the wind, every leaf sharpened to a glass-clear edge by my exhaustion.

I turn my head to watch him. In the last few days he's become not more familiar to me as he should have but more alien. Close up, he's a strange terrain, pores and hairs; but he isn't nearer, he's further away, like the moon when you've finally landed on it. I move back from him so I can see him better; he misinterprets, thinking I'm trying to get up, and stretches himself over me to prevent me. He kisses me, teeth digging into my lower lip; when it hurts too much I pull away. We lie side by side, both suffering from unrequited love.

This is an interval, a truce; it can't last, we both know

it, there have been too many differences, of opinion we called it but it was more than that, the things that mean safety for him mean danger for me. We've talked too much or not enough: for what we have to say to each other there's no language, we've tried them all. I think of the old science-fiction movies, the creature from another galaxy finally encountered after so many years of signals and ordeals only to be destroyed because he can't make himself understood. Actually it's less a truce than a rest, those silent black-and-white comedians hitting each other until they fall down, then getting up after a pause to begin again. We love each other, that's true whatever it means, but we aren't good at it; for some it's a talent, for others only an addiction. I wonder if they ever came here while he was still alive.

Right now though there's neither love nor anger, no resentment, it's a suspension, of fear even, like waiting for the dentist. But I don't want him to die. I feel nothing, but I concentrate, somebody's version of God, I will him to exist, right now on the vacant lawn of this castle whose name we don't know in this foreign town we're in only because dead people are more real to him than living ones. Despite the mistakes I want everything to stay the way it is; I want to hold it.

He sits up: he's heard voices. Two little girls, baskets over their arms as if for a picnic or a game, have come into the grounds and are walking toward the castle. They stare at us curiously and decide we're harmless. "Let's play in the tower," one calls and they run and disappear among the walls. For them the castle is ordinary as a backyard.

He gets up, brushing off bits of grass. We haven't visited the house yet but we still have time. We find our break in the wall, our pathway, and slide back down to sea level. The sun has moved, the green closes behind us.

The house is further than it looked from the village. The semi-road gives out and we pick our way along the stony beach. The tide is out; the huge bay stretches as far as we can see, a solid mud-flat except for the thin silty river that cuts along beside us. The dry part narrows and vanishes, we are stranded below the tide line, clambering over slippery masses of purplish-brown rock or squelching through the mud, thick as clotted cream. All around us is an odd percolating sound: it's the mud, drying in the sun. There are gulls too, and wind bending the unhealthy-coloured rushes by the bank.

"How the hell did he get back and forth?" he says. "Think of doing this drunk on a dark night."

"There must be a road farther up," I say.

We reach the house at last. Like everything else here it has a wall; this one is to keep out the waves at high tide. The house itself is on stilts, jammed up against the cliff, painted stone with a spindly-railed two-decker porch. It hasn't been lived in for many years: one window is broken and the railings are beginning to go. The yard is weed-grown, but maybe it always was.

I sit on the wall, dangling my legs, while he pokes around, examining the windows, the outhouse (which is open), the shed once used perhaps for a boat. I don't want to see any of it. Graves are safely covered and the castle so derelict it has the status of a tree or a stone, but the house is too recent, it's still partly living. If I looked in the window there would be a table with dishes not yet cleared away, or a fresh cigarette or a coat just taken off. Or maybe a broken plate: they used to have fights, apparently. She never comes back and I can see why. He wouldn't leave her alone.

He's testing the railing on the second-storey porch, he's going to pull himself up by it.

"Don't do that," I say wearily.

"Why not?" he says. "I want to see the other side."

"Because you'll fall and I don't want to have to scrape you off the rocks."

"Don't be like that," he says.

How did she manage? I turn my head away, I don't want to watch. It'll be such an effort, the police, I'll have to explain what I was doing here, why he was climbing and fell. He should be more considerate. But for once he thinks better of it.

There's another road, we discover it eventually, along the beach and up an asphalt walk beside a neat inhabited cottage. Did they see us coming, are they wondering who we are? The road above is paved, it has a railing and a sign with the poet's name on it, wired to the fence.

"I'd like to steal that," he says.

We pause to view the house from above. There's an old lady in a garden-party hat and gloves, explaining things to an elderly couple. "He always kept to himself, he did," she is saying. "No-one here ever got to know him really." She goes on to detail the prices that have been offered for the house: America wanted to buy it and ship it across the ocean, she says, but the town wouldn't let them.

We start back toward our room. Halfway along we sit down on a bench to scrape the mud from our boots; it clings like melted marshmallow. I lean back; I'm not sure I can make it to the house, whatever reserves my body has been drawing on are almost gone. My hearing is blurred and it's hard to breathe.

He bends over to kiss me. I don't want him to, I'm not calm now, I'm irritated, my skin prickles, I think of case histories, devoted wives who turn kleptomaniac two days a month, the mother who threw her baby out into the snow, it was in *Readers Digest*, she had a hormone disturbance; love is all chemical. I want it to be over, this long abrasive competition for the role of victim, it used to matter that it should finish right, with grace, but not now. One of us should just get up from the bench, shake hands and leave, I don't care who is last, it would sidestep the recriminations, the totalling-up of scores, the reclaiming of possessions, your key, my book. But it won't be that way, we'll have to work through it, boring and foreordained though it is. What keeps me is a passive curiosity, it's like an Elizabethan tragedy or a horror movie, I know which ones will be killed but not how. I take his hand and stroke the back of it gently, the fine hairs rasping my fingertips like sandpaper.

We'd been planning to change and have dinner, it's almost six, but back in the room I have only strength enough to pull off my boots. Then with my clothes still on I crawl into the enormous, creaking bed, cold as porridge and hammock-saggy. I float for an instant in the open sky on the backs of my eyelids, free fall, until sleep rushes up to meet me like the earth.

I wake up suddenly in total darkness. I remember where I am. He's beside me but he seems to be lying outside the blankets, furled in the bedspread. I get stealthily out of the bed, grope to the window and open one of the wooden shutters. It's almost as dark outside, there are no streetlights, but by straining I can read my watch: two o'clock. I've had my eight hours and my body thinks it's time for breakfast. I notice I still have my clothes on, take them off and get back in bed, but my stomach won't let me sleep. I hesitate, then decide it won't do him any harm and turn on the bedside lamp. On the dresser there's a crumpled paper bag; inside it's a Welsh cake, a soft white biscuit with currants in it. I bought it yesterday near the train station, asking in bakeries crammed with English buns and French pastries, running through the streets in a crazed search for local colour that almost made us late for the bus. Actually I bought two of them. I ate mine yesterday, this one is his, but I don't care; I take it out of the bag and devour it whole.

In the mirror I'm oddly swollen, as if I've been drowned, my eyes are purple-circled, my hair stands out from my head like a second-hand doll's, there's a diagonal scar-like mark across my cheek where I've been sleeping on my face. This is what it does to you. I estimate the weeks, months it will take me to recuperate. Fresh air, good food and plenty of sun.

We have so little time and he just lies there, rolled up like a rug, not even twitching. I think of waking him, I want to make love, I want all there is because there's not much left. I start to think what he'll do after I'm over and I can't stand that, maybe I should kill him, that's a novel idea, how melodramatic; nevertheless I look around the room for a blunt instrument, there's nothing but the bedside lamp, a grotesque woodland nymph with metal tits and a lightbulb coming out of her head. I could never kill anyone with that. Instead I brush my teeth, wondering if he'll ever know how close he came to being murdered, resolving anyway never to plant flowers for him, never to come back, and slide in among the chilly furrows and craters of the bed. I intend to watch the sun rise but I fall asleep by accident and miss it.

Breakfast, when the time for it finally comes, is shabby, decorous, with mended linens and plentiful but dented silver. We have it in an ornate, dilapidated room whose grandiose mantelpiece now supports only china spaniels and tinted family photos. We're brushed and combed, thoroughly dressed; we speak in subdued voices.

The food is the usual, tea and toast, fried eggs and bacon and the inevitable grilled tomato. It's served by a different woman, grey-haired also but with a corrugated perm and red lipstick. We unfold our map and plan the route back; it's Sunday and there won't be a bus to the nearest railway town till after one, we may have trouble getting out.

He doesn't like fried eggs and he's been given two of them. I eat one for him and tell him to hack the other one up so it will look nibbled at least, it's only polite. He's grateful to me, he knows I'm taking care of him, he puts his hand for a moment over mine, the one not holding the fork. We tell each other our dreams: his of men with armbands, later of me in a cage made of frail slat-like bones, mine of escaping in winter through a field.

I eat his grilled tomato as an afterthought and we leave.

Upstairs in our room we pack; or rather I pack, he lies on the bed.

"What're we going to do till the bus comes?" he says. Being up so early unsettles him.

"Go for a walk," I say.

"We went for a walk yesterday," he says.

I turn around and he's holding out his arms, he wants me to come and lie down beside him. I do and he gives me a perfunctory initial kiss and starts to undo my buttons. He's using only his left hand, the right one is underneath me, he's having trouble. I stand up and take off, reluctantly, the clothes I've so recently put on. It's time for sex, he missed out on it last night.

He reaches up and hauls me in among the tangled sheets. I tense; he throws himself on me with the utilitarian urgency of a man running to catch a train, but it's more than that, it's different, he's biting down on my mouth, this time he'll get blood if it kills him. I pull him into me, wanting him to be with me, but for the first time I feel it's just flesh, a body, a beautiful machine, an animated corpse, he isn't in it any more, I want him so much and he isn't here. The bedsprings mourn beneath us.

"Sorry about that," he says.

"It's all right."

"No, shit, I really am sorry. I don't like it when that happens."

"It's all right," I say. I smooth his back, distancing him: he's back by the deserted house, back lying on the grass, back in the graveyard, standing in the sun looking down, thinking of his own death.

"We better get up," I say, "she might want to make up the room."

We're waiting for the bus. They lied to me in the general store, there is a hotel, I can see it now, it's just around the corner. We've had our quarrel, argument, fight, the one we were counting on. It was a routine one, a small one comparatively, its only importance the fact that it was the last. It carries the weight of all the other, larger things we said we forgave each other for but didn't. If there were separate buses we'd take them. As it is we wait together, standing a little apart.

We have over half an hour. "Let's go down to the beach," I say, "we can see the bus from there, it has to go the other way first." I cross the road and he follows me at a distance.

There's a wall; I climb it and sit down. The top is scattered with sharp flakes of broken stone, flint possibly, and bleached thumbnail-sized cockleshells, I know what they are because I saw them in the museum two days ago, and the occasional piece of broken glass. He leans against the wall near me, chewing on a cigarette. We say what we have to say in even, conversational voices, discussing how we'll get back, the available trains. I wasn't expecting it so soon.

After a while he looks at his watch, then walks away from me toward the sea, his boots crunching on the shells and pebbles. At the edge of the reed bank by the river he stops, back to me, one leg slightly bent. He holds his elbows, wrapped in his clothes as if in a cape, the storm breaks, his cape billows, thick leather boots sprout up his legs, a sword springs to attention in his hand. He throws his head back, courage, he'll meet them alone. Flash of lightning. Onward.

I wish I could do it so quickly. I sit calmed, frozen, not yet sure whether I've survived, the words we have hurled at each other lying spread in fragments around me, solidified. It's the pause during the end of the world, how does one behave? The man who said he'd continue to tend his garden, does that make sense to me? It would if it were only a small ending, my own. But we aren't more doomed than anything else, it's dead already, at any moment the bay will vaporize, the hills across will lift into the air, the space between will scroll itself up and vanish; in the graveyard the graves will open to show the dry puffball skulls, his wooden cross will flare like a match, his house collapse into itself, cardboard and lumber, no more language. He will stand revealed, history scaling away from him, the versions of him I made up and applied, stripped down to what he really is for a last instant before he flames up and goes out. Surely we should be holding each other, absolving, repenting, saying goodbye to each other, to everything because we will never find it again.

Above us the gulls wheel and ride, crying like drowning puppies or disconsolate angels. They have black rims around their eyes; they're a new kind, I've never seen any like that before. The tide is going out; the fresh wet mud gleams in the sun, miles of it, a level field of pure glass, pure gold. He stands outlined against it, a dark shape, faceless, light catching the edges of his hair.

I turn aside and look down at my hands. They are covered with greyish dust: I've been digging among the shells, gathering them together. I arrange them in a border, a square, each white shell overlapping the next. Inside I plant the flints, upright in tidy rows, like teeth, like flowers.

LEO SIMPSON was born in 1934 in Limerick, where he spent most of his childhood in hospital. He came to Canada as a young man, and has been able to make a living as a free-lance writer since 1966. He is the author of *Arkwright*, and is working on a second novel, *The Peacock Papers*. He has also written several plays for the CBC and reviews for the Toronto *Globe*. Despite internal evidence, he claims that he no longer writes stories, since there is no market for them.

JANE RULE was born in New Jersey in 1931, and is a Canadian citizen, living now in Vancouver. She has published three novels, is working on another, as well as some stories and "diatribes." She teaches intermittently at UBC.

JOHN NEWLOVE was born in Regina in 1938 and has lived mostly in Saskatchewan and British Columbia, though he now lives in Toronto and works for McClelland and Stewart. He has published two collections of poems, *Black Night Window* and *The Cave*, and is currently writing both poetry and stories.

DON BAILEY was born in Toronto in 1942, spent five years in jail, and now works at the Christian Resource Centre in Toronto. He is an indefatigable writer and is at the moment finishing a novel, *Allegiances*, and bringing together a collection of stories and a new book of poems.

GEORGE MCWHIRTER is an Ulsterman by birth and a Canadian by adoption. He teaches in the creative-writing program at the University of British Columbia. His first book, *Catalan Poems* was published last year and he is now working on a collection of stories.

BETH HARVOR was born in Saint John, NB in 1936 and has had her stories published in numerous periodicals, largely in the United States. "The Magicians" won a prize from CBC Ottawa but hasn't yet been broadcast.

JOHN SANDMAN was born in 1948 and recently received a Canada Council arts bursary and an Ontario Arts Council grant. Before that he worked in the Ontario stockyards, driving cattle. He is the author of *Eating Out* and is busy working on two novels and several stories.

NORA KEELING was born in Owen Sound in 1933 and lived for some time in France and England, though she returned to Ontario some years ago. She is working on a book of stories.

ANDREAS SCHROEDER was born in Germany in 1946, and is currently at UBC. He has published two books of poetry and worked as a book and magazine editor and translator from both French and German.

GAIL FOX was born in 1942 and studied music at Cornell. She is the author of *Dangerous Season* and *The Royal Collector of Dreams*, both books of poetry, and her contribution to this year's anthology is one of the first stories she has written.

DAVID MCFADDEN was born in Hamilton in 1940 and has lived and worked there all his life. He has published both poetry and fiction, and is currently working on a new book of poems called *Sentimental Slop*.

MARGARET ATWOOD was born in Ottawa in 1939 and now lives in Toronto. Her novel, *The Edible Woman*, is shortly to be filmed, with Tony Richardson directing. She won the Governor General's Award for *The Circle Game*, and has written several volumes of poetry. A new novel, *Forehead Eye*, will appear in September 1972.

DAVID HELWIG teaches English at Queen's University. He is the author of two books of poetry and one of stories. His first novel, *The Day Before Tomorrow* was published in 1971, and a new collection of poetry, *The Best Name of Silence*, will appear in September 1972.

JOAN HARCOURT is a Canadian who lived for many years in England, where she was a reader for various film companies and a book reviewer for a pacifist weekly. She is now an editor at McGill-Queen's University Press.